St. Sebastian's Church

Knight Street

Lawton Square

Boston, Mass.

June Street

Bishop Street

#224 Knight St.
Zanna's Grandmother's House

Kingston Boulevard

The
MASTERMIND PLOT

ANGIE FRAZIER

SCHOLASTIC PRESS / NEW YORK

Library of Congress Cataloging-in-Publication Data
Frazier, Angie.
The Mastermind Plot / by Angie Frazier. — 1st ed.
p. cm.
Sequel to: The midnight tunnel
Summary: In 1904, eleven-year-old Suzanna is delighted with her grandmother's invitation to spend
time in Boston and thrilled to help her famous uncle investigate a series of arsons, but much less
pleased to be enrolled in Miss Lydia Doucette's Academy for Young Ladies.
[1. Mystery and detective stories. 2. Arson — Fiction. 3. Private schools — Fiction. 4. Schools — Fiction.
5. Family life — Massachusetts — Boston — Fiction. 6. Uncles — Fiction. 7. Grandmothers — Fiction.
8. Boston (Mass.) — History — 20th century — Fiction.] I. Title.
PZ7.F8688Suz 2012
[Fic] — dc22
2011003770

ISBN 978-0-545-20864-2

10 9 8 7 6 5 4 3 2 1   12 13 14 15 16

Printed in the U.S.A.   23
First edition, March 2012

The text was set in ITC Esprit.
Endpaper map art © by Mike Schley
Book design by Lillie Howard

For my grandparents,
Bernard and Natalie Robie
and
Francis and Marieta Hall
With much love

Chapter One

• • •

Sat., Sept. 12, 1904: Train is about to arrive in Boston. Condition of hands: sweating. Heart: pounding. Legs: cramping.

• • •

EVERYONE WITHIN SIGHT WAS A SUSPECT. THERE was no question about it. With such frowns and long faces, the passengers in my rattling railway car just had to be guilty of something. No one wore a smile. Well, no one but me, of course, and I had a very good reason to smile. In about ten minutes, my lifelong dream would come true.

I'd be in Boston, the place I'd wanted to be for as long as I could remember. My uncle, the famous detective Bruce Snow, lived and worked here, and it would be here, in Boston, where I would become a true detective. I simply had to. I couldn't bear to return home, to the boring little seaside town of Loch Harbor, New Brunswick, without some sort of detective training.

I closed my notebook and set it back inside my cloak's wide pocket. I kept a notebook with me always, along with a pencil and silver pocket watch to record exact time logs. This was a new notebook, the last one chockful of the notes, observations, theories, time lines, and clues I'd gathered during my very first case over the summer. I'd helped solve the disappearance of a little girl from Boston who'd been staying at the Rosemount, my parents' hotel. It wasn't supposed to have been my case, though. Everyone had expected Uncle Bruce to get the job done. And in the end, he *had* been the one to reunite Maddie Cook and her mother (with overly dramatic flair, I might add) in front of all the guests. But he hadn't closed the case on his own, and soon enough, all the guests had learned of my role — and then all the Boston newspapers had as well.

My true detective training would require Uncle Bruce to actually spend time with me. Hope for that was slim, however, considering he hadn't been the one to invite me to Boston. My father's mother, the grandmother I'd only met twice and had little memory of, had sent the invitation. I wished it had been from Uncle Bruce, but to him, I, Suzanna Snow, was nothing but the pesky eleven-year-old girl who'd undermined his case at the Rosemount and had made a fool of him.

Still, I clung to a thread of hope that he'd forgotten all of that. I huffed lightly to myself as the train started to slow. And maybe he'd magically sprouted wings and a tail and had turned into a Pegasus as well. It was just as likely.

In the seat beside me, Nellie, the Rosemount's irritable cook, flipped up the collar of her tweed coat and scowled out the foggy window.

"As if I didn't have plenty of other things to do this week than bring you all the way down to this dreadful place," Nellie muttered, tucking her thin frame down into her bulky overcoat.

My parents had asked Nellie to be my traveling chaperone since neither of them could take the time away from the hotel. The Rosemount had closed for the season but there were still plenty of duties to see to. Endless, tedious tasks my parents took to with an enthusiasm I had never been able to muster.

"Boston isn't dreadful. It's lively and modern, and people love it here," I replied. I had no solid proof for any of those claims, but I believed what I said. If Boston wasn't wonderful, why would so many people live here?

Nellie huffed out a mirthless laugh. "It was dreadful enough for your parents to move away and never go back. Your father was against this trip right from the start, and I'm sure he had reliable reasons."

I sat back in my green velour seat. At first, it hadn't struck me as odd when Father had immediately said no to the trip. For reasons I was now beginning to understand, my father didn't particularly like his brother. Besides, there was a lot of work to be done at the Rosemount, even during the off-season. Father depended on me, he'd claimed. His rare compliment had nearly caused me to stop being angry over his refusal to let me go to Boston.

But then he and Mother had continued to argue for days after Grandmother's letter arrived. Mother had been all for my visit, saying they couldn't keep me away forever, that my grandmother deserved to get to know me. Father had said it was "too dangerous," an exact quote I'd heard through the floor grates one night after they believed I'd gone to bed. (Spying was, by far, the best part of detective work.)

I didn't understand what could be so dangerous about Boston. It was just a place. And considering he and Mother had both grown up there and turned out just fine, what possible damage could a two-month stay at my grandmother's do?

The train blared out its arrival whistle. The screeching of metal and brakes and the hiss of steam blended with the uproar of the passengers rustling about in their seats. Nellie and I had left Loch Harbor's station early the day before and had run down the coast of New Brunswick, through the dense forests and open farmlands of Maine, along the brief New Hampshire seacoast, and into the northern edge of Massachusetts, where there was a constant panorama of brick mills and smokestacks.

I itched to fetch my carrying bag from the gold barred rack above our heads and to get off the train. White blasts of steam clouded the air outside. All I could glimpse through the windows was the pitched roof of the station and a hazy mass of people milling about the platform — which was about ten times the size of Loch Harbor's.

At last the train came to a full stop. I flew to my feet and grabbed for my bags. Nellie took her time standing, stretching, and repositioning her burgundy pillbox hat. She then slowly re-pinned a few stray wisps of coarse, grayish-brown hair. I knew Nellie hadn't wanted to see me down to Boston, but she hadn't been able to say no to my parents. Nellie had exactly two soft spots, and they were reserved for Cecilia and Benjamin Snow.

I ran a hand over my own hair — two pale brown braids that reached just barely to my shoulders. I suddenly longed for a better, more mature hairstyle. I made a mental note to get rid of my childish braids before I saw my uncle.

Nellie and I followed the herd of others down the aisle and out onto the platform. One good thing about Nellie was how efficient she was. Within a minute she'd spotted our cases in the growing pile of luggage being dragged off the train. And then, with her tall, lanky height, she craned her neck above the sea of heads and saw Grandmother's driver holding up a sign that read *Snow*, as if he was calling for a change in weather.

"Don't dawdle, now," Nellie said. She cut a path through the crowd, her hand raised to flag the driver.

I kept close behind for fear I'd become lost in the chaos. As the steam cleared from the air, the noises of the depot took over. People rushed around, their hands and arms gesturing this way and that, their shoulders bumping into backs and legs into luggage, and the noise . . . it was so loud I wanted to cover my ears.

The driver retrieved our luggage and swept us away to a covered carriage beside the depot. He loaded our things on the roof while Nellie and I sat inside. The brisk air snapped at my nose as I leaned my head out the open window and stared into the swarm of people.

I squinted against the sunlight blurring my vision. I was just about to turn away and blink back the tears when something stole my attention. Some*one*, actually. A tall, lean man with broad shoulders stood by a lamppost two buggy lengths ahead of us. He pulled his crisp, black, brimmed hat lower over his forehead, but his sharp eyes were unmistakably fixed on Grandmother's carriage. He wasn't just staring at the carriage, though. He was staring at *me*. His eyes were searing and hard, his cheekbones defined, and his chin pointed.

I reached out and tugged on Nellie's coat sleeve without breaking from his harsh gaze.

"Nellie, why do you think that man's staring this way?"

"Good lord, child." Nellie plucked her sleeve out of my grasp. "Who's who? I see more people out there than every citizen in the whole of Loch Harbor."

The buggy ahead of us pulled out, led by two harnessed gray mares. By the time it drove away, the space by the lamppost was empty.

"Never mind," I said.

The strange man with the inquisitive eyes was gone.

• • •

Our carriage swerved down cluttered streets. Each second, my ears were assaulted by a new sound: the blare of a police whistle, the shouting of children on corners, the *clop-clopping* of horse hooves, and the screech of metal on metal as trains rattled by on tracks raised all the way up near the peaks of houses. I stared

7

openmouthed as they rumbled overhead, feeling as if I'd been transported to a futuristic world. Even Nellie looked pleasantly astounded, and I wondered if she was rethinking her earlier judgment of Boston.

The carriage turned, shot through a narrow side street, and then came back out onto another street, this one lined with trees, the leaves all speckled with the first hints of fall. The branches reached out over the street, creating a massive, ongoing bough overhead as we rolled down a slight hill. Here, stately brick-fronted homes were enclosed by wrought-iron fences, one right after the other. A cobbled sidewalk trimmed each side of the street.

"Knight Street," the driver hollered back.

Grandmother's street! My heart lifted, shaking off the stress of the last handful of streets. Father had said Grandmother lived in a neighborhood called Lawton Square, and that Boston was made up of many different neighborhoods. Lawton Square alone, he'd told me, was about the size of Loch Harbor. So Boston itself was like dozens of Loch Harbors all squished together. I had to admit that the idea of that was a little overwhelming.

At least Knight Street was slow and elegant. I sighed as the carriage stopped outside a brownstone, the sandstone blocks the color of chocolate. The shutters were painted a deep, earthy red, and the glass windows gleamed in the late afternoon light where thick leaves did not cast their shadows. A polished brass plate had been fixed above the front door and engraved with the numbers 224. *224 Knight Street*. The address had a dignified ring to it, much like 221B Baker Street, which was, of course, the London residence of one of my favorite fictional detectives, Sherlock Holmes.

I climbed out of the carriage behind Nellie. The short heel of one of my boots immediately sank between two cobblestones and became wedged there. I tugged at it until it came free, and stumbled forward. My shins bumped into the large trunk that the driver had fetched down, and to no surprise, I lost my balance. Unfortunately, the moment my hands and knees slammed against the cobble sidewalk, I also heard my name being called.

"Suzanna?"

I peered up from my ridiculous position in front of Grandmother's house, and shoved my braids back from where they swung before my eyes. In front of me stood a tall, robust man in a long coat made of dark broadcloth.

"Uncle Bruce!"

I quickly got to my feet. Uncle Bruce's thick

mustache prickled like quills as he regarded me and forced a smile.

"I am stunned to see you here. I do not understand the meaning of it," he said, the cadence of his voice strained and overly proper.

A tall, thin man with a square jaw stood just behind Uncle Bruce. He was clean-shaven, with a pale complexion and a few wisps of light blond hair that hung down across his forehead. He inspected me from behind a pair of wire-rimmed eyeglasses before turning a vexed look toward Uncle Bruce, as if bothered by my uncle's rude greeting.

Uncle Bruce didn't bother to introduce me.

"I received an invitation," I said.

Uncle Bruce ripped off his hat. His dark, glossy hair fell in front of his brown eyes, which were currently simmering with discontent. "An invitation? From whom?"

"From me."

Uncle Bruce, Nellie, and I spun toward the town house. Standing in the doorway was a short, rotund woman. Gaudy rings and bracelets dwarfed her already small hands, which were clasped in front of her obviously corseted waist. I stood a good ten feet away, but her bright, ice blue eyes struck me at once. They were my father's eyes.

"Mother, you — you —" Uncle Bruce sputtered.

My grandmother's powdery white face, pinched with just two spots of color on her cheekbones, crinkled up into a smile. "Yes, Bruce. Me."

She took the steps down toward the wrought-iron gate with more elegance than even my mother might have managed. Needless to say, I was immediately terrified.

"Darling Suzanna!" Grandmother held out her petite arms toward me. She looked as if she was going to walk straight into the gate. Uncle Bruce quickly reached down and unlatched it, and I realized Grandmother had expected him to do no less.

"Welcome to Boston, dear. I can't tell you what a joy it is to finally see you again." She grinned warmly and caught both of my arms in her birdlike hands. She gave them a delicate squeeze, then glanced sideways at Uncle Bruce. Her blue eyes glittered with what I detected as mischief.

"Am I to assume you object to our Suzanna's visit?" she asked.

Nellie harrumphed, already aware of his prickly personality from the time he spent at the Rosemount. Uncle Bruce's mustache seemed to come to life again, twitching and wriggling as he prepared to answer.

"No, no," he finally said. He tugged his hat back on. "I am delighted, Suzanna, to have you here with us."

His fiery eyes and sour grimace couldn't hide anything. Uncle Bruce was livid. And he wasn't delighted to have me here at all.

Chapter Two

• • •

Mental Note: Wire-rimmed eyeglasses make one look exceptionally intelligent. Must complain of eyestrain and convince Grandmother to purchase me a pair.

• • •

A YOUNG WOMAN WITH HARDLY ANY CHIN closed the frosted-glass door behind us and helped me out of my traveling cloak. I stood rigid, not used to being the object of a servant's attention. She turned me out of my cloak and freed me of my gloves in a blur of motion, and then moved on to help Nellie. I was left a bit dazed from such efficiency, but followed my grandmother as she glided into a sitting room.

I stepped inside and abruptly stopped, stunned. The walls, papered in a busy floral design, were covered from base to ceiling with plates, mirrors, silhouettes, paintings, and sketches. A massive grandfather clock filled a corner; a glassed-in curio cabinet displayed trinkets and more ceramics; tables seemed to be everywhere, forming a maze of sorts; long, heavy drapes brushed the floors, which were covered in Oriental rugs; and sconces, dripping with sparkling crystal beads, were mounted on each wall.

Never before had I seen a room like it. Not even at the Rosemount, where antlers and snowshoes and bearskins draped the walls of the Great Hall. Grandmother's parlor made my head spin with all of its . . . *clutter.*

She seated herself in a lavender-colored chair, the velvet upholstery so plush I feared she might disappear right into it.

"Do sit, dear," she said to me. I picked a more solid-looking chair near a writing desk. She frowned at my choice.

Uncle Bruce came inside the parlor, another false smile fixed on his lips. "Mother, you were quite silent about this invitation to my niece."

He'd done that back in Loch Harbor, too — speaking about me as though I wasn't right there in the room with him.

Nellie came into the parlor looking a bit flustered from the servant girl's lightning-quick hands. Uncle Bruce's silent companion followed.

"Bruce, dear, it's been far too long since I've seen my granddaughter. Besides, the papers were all raving about Suzanna's heroics regarding that little missing girl. I found myself quite jealous that the reporters seemed to know her better than I did! It was utterly unacceptable."

She glanced at me. Her eyes were so like my father's. I felt a deep tug in my stomach. Homesickness. I'd promised myself I wouldn't be homesick, and shoved it down.

"Darling, how was your trip? Miss Bridges, was it terribly uncomfortable?"

It took me a second to understand that she was addressing Nellie. No one back home ever used her last name. She was the only Nellie in Loch Harbor.

"No more uncomfortable than standing on my feet all day in a hot kitchen," Nellie replied as she perched herself on the edge of a curvy sofa. She'd never been one to mince words. I drew up my shoulders and looked nervously to my grandmother for her reaction. She had on a sympathetic pout.

"Of course not. Benjamin writes so highly of your abilities. He and Cecilia must think of you superiorly to trust you with the care of their daughter."

Nellie weighed my grandmother's compliment with plain skepticism. After an awkward moment, she said, "Well, the feelings are mutual. I think the world of Mr. and Mrs. Snow."

I waited for Nellie to say something kind about me but knew it was in vain.

Grandmother then turned toward my uncle. "Now, Bruce, you don't usually pay me visits on Tuesday afternoons. To what do I owe this pleasure? And good afternoon to you, Detective Grogan."

She cleared her throat, clearly wanting Uncle Bruce to introduce Detective Grogan to me. The title *detective* intrigued me and I immediately set about inspecting him. He was tall, like my uncle, but not as robust. His frame was more streamlined and wiry, like his eyeglasses.

"Good afternoon, Mrs. Snow." His voice did not match him at all. It was a raspy, deep tenor, nearly as burly as Uncle Bruce's. I must have startled with surprise, because he glanced my way.

"And to you as well, Miss Snow. It's a pleasure to meet you. I'm Detective Neil Grogan." He dipped into a gentlemanly bow. On rising to his full height again, he added, "I was sorry to miss the investigation in Loch Harbor. I'm told you did a dandy of a job finding that young girl."

He tipped his head toward me in a sign of respect. I beamed with surprise.

"Thank you, it's nice to meet you —"

Uncle Bruce cleared his throat to drown me out. "Yes, well, Neil, I was sorry to have gone to my brother's hotel without you. I had young Will with me, of course, but the boy left me wanting for someone with more extensive field experience."

I bit the inside of my cheek to keep from arguing. Will, my cousin and Uncle Bruce's apprentice over the summer, had been more than helpful. Will and I, not Uncle Bruce, had found little Maddie Cook. From the corner of my vision, I thought I saw Grandmother roll her eyes. But when I looked again, she was sitting primly and smiling at Uncle Bruce.

"And so why have you ambled up to Lawton Square this afternoon, Bruce?" she asked, redirecting her point.

"It's nothing, Mother. It can wait until after you've helped Suzanna settle in."

He took a sidelong glance at me. It hit like a blast of hot steam from the train.

Detective Grogan stepped forward. "I might have discovered some similarities between the Horne fires and an older case, one that Bruce worked on when he was a rookie. He said you might still have some of his things from those days. Notebooks and such."

I stared at my uncle. Notebooks? Notebooks like mine? Uncle Bruce directed his eyes toward the ceiling, avoiding my glance.

Grandmother leaned forward. "An older case? Well, I don't know. . . . I might still have a few boxes of his things in the basement." She pinched her lips together, inspected my uncle, and no doubt saw his cross expression. "But I most likely don't, Detective Grogan. And my son is right — I really must attend to my granddaughter at the moment. Perhaps Bruce could come back and have a look around himself?"

The Horne fires. An older case. Notebooks filled with observations and clues. My interest was officially hooked. I watched as Uncle Bruce's stiff shoulders loosened.

"Excellent idea, Mother. We'll be off." He went to his mother's chair and delivered a hasty peck to her cheek.

Uncle Bruce swept out into the foyer. Detective Grogan, looking somewhat crestfallen at not being able to search for those old notebooks, at least had the decency to give another short bow to Nellie and me before leaving.

Something in the way Detective Grogan had held himself apart from Uncle Bruce, and especially in the way he'd complimented me, gave me the notion that he had been trying to twist a thorn in his partner's side. I immediately approved of him.

Nellie sighed to break up the new silence. In any other company, she would have made a comment about Uncle Bruce's poor behavior. But she kept her thin lips sealed, with only a sharp glance at Grandmother.

"Please don't mind Bruce. He has always found it difficult to give credit where credit is due." Grandmother winked at me. "I spoke with Will just after he and Bruce arrived home in July, and he told me everything you did, Suzanna. And then the papers were all raving about you. I can't tell you how proud I was to hear of it all."

The serving girl had come into the parlor with tea. She handed me a full cup. I was so excited to hear Will's name that I nearly spilled it.

"He did? How is he? Will I see him?"

Grandmother chuckled over my eagerness to see my cousin.

"I'm sure you will, and very soon. But I first plan to be very selfish — I want you all to myself, my dear. It's been years since I've seen you."

At least five, I calculated, vaguely remembering her last visit. I also had fuzzy memories of my grandfather, though he'd passed away a year or two after their last trip to Loch Harbor. My father had gone to Boston for the funeral, alone, my mother explaining that the train ride was long and that funerals were often too sad for children. Grandmother had continued to send me cards and presents at my birthdays and holidays, but she didn't like traveling alone. And my parents didn't like traveling *at all*.

Grandmother continued, "I'm sorry your uncle seemed exasperated by your arrival. I'm afraid he has been under an enormous amount of pressure lately."

I took a scalding sip of tea and burned off half of my taste buds.

"What are the Horne fires?" I asked. I patted my skirt for my notebook but remembered it was in my cloak pocket. I'd have to memorize Grandmother's answer instead.

"Just some local troubles, dear. A few warehouses owned by a Boston businessman have gone up in flames. Bruce seems to be having an uncommonly hard time with the investigation." Grandmother took up her tea after stirring in a cube of sugar. "But we'll have no unpleasant talk this afternoon."

It wouldn't have been unpleasant talk for me. But I supposed Grandmother was a lady, and most ladies would have thought arson a rude subject. Grandmother rose up from her seat and abandoned her tea. She crossed the room toward me, and in a sudden gesture of enthusiasm, took my cheeks into her warm hands. Her eyes danced with delight.

"How splendid this autumn is going to be with you here, Zanna!"

I blinked a few times, surprised she was already using my nickname.

"That is what your friends call you, is it not?" she asked. "Will told me you prefer it."

I nodded, again looking forward to seeing Will. Grandmother let go of my cheeks and stepped back, her gaze turning serious.

"We must settle you into your room before the seamstress arrives to fit you for an academy uniform. Come, como."

She started for the foyer. I set my full cup down, splashing some steaming tea onto the saucer.

"Academy?" My parents had said I'd most likely have a tutor for the few months I'd be in Boston.

Grandmother's extreme hourglass figure twisted as she looked back at me. "I've decided to enroll you in the best academy in all of Boston, and it just so happens to be right here, in Lawton Square. Your education will not be neglected under *my* watchful eye." Grandmother smiled, obviously pleased with herself.

Nellie made an approving noise from her seat on the sofa. "And hopefully it will hold the girl's interest better than the school in Loch Harbor did."

I couldn't help it if school was a bore. Given the choice between learning arithmetic and learning how to handcuff a criminal, I'd choose handcuffs every time.

Grandmother straightened the tapered sleeves of her frilly dress. "Oh, it most certainly will interest her. Miss Doucette has the finest reputation here in the city."

My pulse streamed out an extra few beats. "Miss Doucette?"

Maddie Cook had once bragged about attending a marvelous academy and *Doucette* rang a bell.

"Yes. You'll be starting first thing on Monday at Miss Lydia Doucette's Academy for Young Ladies."

Chapter Three

• • •

The clever combatant imposes his will on the enemy, but does not allow the enemy's will to be imposed on him. — Sun Tzu, Chinese general.

• • •

THE SHARP TWANG OF HARP STRINGS, THE bubbly roll of piano keys, and the hollow breath of flutes filled the music room inside Miss Lydia Doucette's Academy for Young Ladies on Monday afternoon. I sat in a cushioned chair as far into the corner of the room as possible, and partly behind the floor-length drapes. My first day at the academy had proved as wretched as I'd anticipated. Right when Grandmother's carriage had rolled up beside the four-story, Gothic-style schoolhouse on Graylock Road, which was only three blocks from 224 Knight Street, my stomach had flipped like one of the Bay of Fundy's porpoises. And I'd been correct to be nervous.

Though Miss Lydia Doucette had greeted Nellie and me in the foyer with warmth, my introduction to the academy girls had been awkward, to say the least. The girls looked to range from age six to sixteen, and nearly all of them had stared at me with awestruck expressions when Miss Doucette ushered me into a classroom with rows of wooden desks, as if I was some sort of circus freak. Nellie had left almost immediately to go to the depot and return home as planned, and I'd been tempted to beg her to take me with her.

One girl acted differently, though. She sat at the center desk in the second row, her posture perfect, her glossy black curls loose around her shoulders. Her bright, gray eyes had immediately caught mine and held me in their clutches. Her stare had not been the mesmerized one plastered to the rest of the faces in the room, but one of loathing and suspicion. It seemed I'd already made my second enemy in Boston, and I couldn't form a single theory as to how I'd done it.

Music was, thankfully, the last lesson of the day. After French, geometry, European literature, and composition, my head felt stuffed with all sorts of knowledge I feared I wouldn't remember the next day. The cold, silver-plated flute slipped around in my sweaty palms as I fiddled with it in my lap. My fingers tapped ignorantly at the keys along the top of the instrument. Everyone was expected to learn a musical instrument, and right then we were supposed to be warming up for lessons. I was too mortified to even lift the flute to my lips for a test blow.

A girl, perhaps a year or two younger than me, slid into the chair next to mine. She held a flute as well and brought it up to her mouth as if she was going to play. But then she jerked her chair closer to mine and surprised me with a whisper.

"You're the one from the papers, aren't you?" If she'd meant to be covert, she would need to try harder next time. Everyone in the row in front of us turned around to listen in.

It was the first anyone, other than Miss Doucette, had spoken to me all day. I'd assumed everyone was uncomfortable with the subject of little Maddie Cook — she could no longer attend such an illustrious academy now that Mr. Cook was in prison and his fortune had been dashed to the wind.

"I suppose I am," I answered, hesitant. Maddie had been found because of me, yes. But she was also no longer at the academy because of me.

I'd discovered her brother and father had been attempting to carry out a wretched crime that involved stealing from a longtime guest of the Rosemount. Would these girls be upset with me for it? Was that why the black-haired girl had been sneering at me all day? Her name, I'd learned, was Adele, and just then she sat behind one of the two harps in the music room.

"So you really did find Maddie Cook locked up in a cellar hole on an uninhabited island?" the girl asked, breathless. The other girls leaned toward me in their chairs, waiting for my reply.

What sort of rubbish had those newspapers printed?

"Locked up in a cellar hole?" I repeated. "Of course not. She was perfectly fine. Some old hermit lady had been taking care of her."

The girls' shoulders slumped with unanimous disappointment. Apparently, the truth wasn't as exciting as what they'd been led to believe.

Adele's lithe fingers strummed the harp's strings with elegant strokes. She was pinning me once again with one of her scathing glares. I'd shrunk back from them all day, but now I was starting to get angry — and inquisitive. Why exactly was this girl so upset with me? The others seemed to just be curious and apprehensive.

Miss Doucette entered the room. Her long yellow bell-shaped skirt sported a large bustle in the back, making her look like a queen bee. The black lace around her collar and wrists and down the front of her dress helped the look along. She clapped her bony hands.

"All right, girls. Turn to page fourteen in your music books, the Chopin nocturne."

All of the girls flipped through a thick book of sheet music set upon their stands. I took a glance around my stand and feet, but I had no such book. Of course I didn't. Instead, I had to raise my hand and draw attention to myself. Miss Doucette craned her neck to see me.

"Yes, Suzanna?"

"I don't have sheet music," I answered sheepishly.

Miss Doucette shuffled around a few music stands but didn't find an extra.

"Oh, dear," she murmured. "Well, you must have sheet music, and if you share with another flutist, you'll be quite in her way. I suppose you simply must go up to the attic where the extra music books are stored. Do I have a volunteer to show Suzanna the way?"

I jumped from my seat. "I can find it on my own."

How perfect! If I tarried long enough, I could miss ten minutes or more of the music lesson. I'd prefer the whole hour, but I'd take what I could get.

Miss Doucette pulled out a big metal ring that held a dozen or more skeleton keys. They slid along the ring until she held one of them up.

"It's the second door on the right on the fourth floor. You'll find the music books in a trunk just inside the attic. Hurry now," she said. I set down my flute and happily crossed the room to take the key.

Three sets of stairs later, all climbed at a leisurely pace, I found myself at the door that led up into the attic. I inserted the key and twisted the lock. There was a narrow set of steps ahead of me. Daylight spilled through the attic windows and lit up the dust motes hanging in the air.

Once at the top, I saw five or six trunks piled right next to the steps, as Miss Doucette had directed. The search for a music book would definitely take me more than the ten minutes I'd been hoping for. Giddy with such luck, I ran my hand over the top of one of the trunks and gathered a mitten of dust on my palm.

Dust floated up into my nostrils. Just as I stifled a sneeze, I heard the sharp bang of the attic door. I went to the top of the steps, saw the door had been shut, and then heard the distinct click of the lock. The key — I'd left it hanging in the lock.

I shot down the steps and tried the handle, but it didn't budge.

"Open the door!" I shouted.

A purring laugh came from the other side.

"I said open the door. This isn't funny!"

The laugh halted. "You rescued Maddie, didn't you? Let's see how well you do at rescuing yourself."

Adele. It had to be her. Somehow she'd followed me.

"Best of luck," she said with false sweetness. Her shoes tapped quickly back down the hallway.

I jiggled the door handle a few more times, but it was useless. That monster! I pounded the door, thinking to shout loud enough to get someone's attention. I stopped to listen and could barely hear the tinkling of the piano and the trill of the flutes already playing. They'd never hear me above their music, and at such a distance.

I turned around and went back up the steps. It didn't matter. After fifteen minutes Miss Doucette would either send someone to find me or come herself. I could just picture Adele sitting behind her harp, smirking with satisfaction when I was finally freed from the attic and marched back down to the music room in humiliation. I couldn't allow it to happen, and definitely not on my very first day. I had to show that Adele girl who she was dealing with.

I went to the tall window and looked out over the horizon of trees, brick buildings, chimney stacks, and in the distance, open water. I was willing to bet Uncle Bruce would never find himself locked in an attic somewhere. I fiddled with the iron latch on the window. Now if I could somehow get out of the attic without needing to scream for help . . . if I could miraculously walk back into the music room with my sheet music in hand as if nothing had ever occurred. Now, that would send Adele's smug look straight into the gutter.

Outside the window a few pigeons roosted along the trim of the attic turret. One pigeon fluttered onto a tall, curved handle sticking up over the edge of the parapet. There were two of these curved iron handles. I caught my breath and pressed my face closer to the window. Was it a fire escape ladder?

I unlocked the window latch, threw up the sash, and stuck my head as far out as possible. I could see a few of the metal rungs below, but that was all. I'd need a better view. The only way to get it would be to crawl out onto the two-foot-wide parapet with the roosting pigeons.

"Zanna, don't be stupid," I whispered to myself. But time was ticking away and soon Miss Doucette would be looking for me. I couldn't let Adele humiliate me.

I rushed back to the trunks and flung them all open. I saw the music books at last, and grabbed one before going back to the window. My throat cinched tight when I glanced down and saw the tops of the maple trees below. Taking a deep breath, I nudged my knee up onto the windowsill and pulled myself out onto the sloped steeple edge.

As I lowered my feet and braced them against the slight upward curve of the copper gutter, I pressed my spine and shoulders back against the steeple's slope. I then slid, slowly, to the left, toward the iron handles of the ladder. The pigeons there cooed and took flight. Biting down on the music book so I could have two free hands, I grasped the handles of the ladder, which were rusty with disuse and age.

Sweating despite the brisk wind, I peeked over the edge. The rungs went all the way down to the second floor, where the escape ladder became a much safer version, with stairs and platforms. If I could just get to the second story, I'd be set. I could sneak inside through the back door that we'd used for our constitutional stroll after luncheon.

The wind ruffled my uniform skirt as I slid my legs out over the ladder and slowly twisted around to descend. If anyone saw me right then, I'd be just as humiliated as I would be if found locked in the attic.

I felt for the next rung down, my teeth biting hard into the music book. The paper tasted moldy, but it didn't matter as much as needing both of my hands to guide me down. Rung after rung passed under my feet, and my heartbeat began to slow. One story of windows came and went, and I sped up my descent. I'd been gone from the music room at least ten minutes, if not more.

As my boot came down onto the next rung, an unnamable sensation swept over me. I knew — just knew — that someone was watching me. I turned my head and looked down. That was my first mistake. My vision spun out of control, the trees and surrounding buildings tipping and blurring together. My vision had barely settled when my eyes landed on the same man who had been watching me at the depot the day before. He stood behind the wrought-iron fence that bordered the academy's back courtyard and stared up at me with a quizzical frown.

I jumped with surprise and rattled the ladder — that was my second mistake. My lower boot slipped off the rung and I dropped, my hands sliding painfully down the rusty iron handles. I yelped and the music book fell from my teeth.

I thought I heard the stranger shout, "No!" but it was lost in the panicked rush of blood through my ears.

My upper boot slipped off the rung and now I was left dangling ten feet over the platform below. I kicked around to find another rung, but connected with nothing but air. The cold iron was fast numbing my hands. My weight was too much for my arms to support. I screamed as my fingers slipped from the bars. Wind rushed up my skirt and a second later, my feet hit the metal platform of the second story.

I collapsed onto my side, the breath knocked from my lungs. *That* had certainly not been part of my revenge plan. As quickly as my aching limbs could take me, I got to my feet. The stranger had jumped the fence and was running across the back courtyard, his long black overcoat flapping out behind him. He paused as soon as he saw me stand, uninjured in any noticeable way.

I met his eyes, the question of who he was and why he was following me on the tip of my tongue. But I hesitated. When he looked at me with that expression of concern, it was so very familiar. Fear and anger and frustration all wrapped up into one penetrating stare.

He covered his eyes with a tug of his black hat's brim and started back for the fence, pulling his overcoat together to button it.

"No, wait!" I shouted.

He increased his speed, his build rather athletic for an older gentleman. But how could he be a gentleman if he was following an eleven-year-old girl around Boston? He swung himself over the fence with ease and disappeared just as I heard the back door to the academy fly open.

"Who is out here?" Miss Doucette's shrill voice called. She couldn't see me from where the fire escape was located on the side of the building. But my music book lay open on the grass, and Miss Doucette rushed over to pick it up. She spied me on the platform above her and screamed with alarm.

"Suzanna!" She clutched at her chest. "What are you doing up there?"

A stream of green-and-navy-blue-plaid-uniformed girls followed until every last one of them, including Adele, was staring up at me in amused shock.

"I, um . . . I just . . ." My plans to thwart Adele crumbled around me, leaving me feeling bare and miserable and pathetic. What was I to do, accuse Adele of locking me in the attic? Miss Doucette would have scoffed at that, and besides, I wasn't going to rat.

"I locked myself in the attic by accident," I finally answered. Adele's leering grin reversed into a look of surprise.

"How did you manage to do that?" Miss Doucette asked, incredulous as she approached the bottom of the fire escape and pulled down the final portion of ladder.

"I don't know." I climbed down the metal steps, my left ankle aching. "I left the key in the lock and I shut the door, and . . . I don't know how I did it, Miss Doucette. I'm sorry."

The girls giggled as I climbed down to the perfection of solid ground. Miss Doucette reprimanded me for not staying put, for not shouting for help, and for taking such an unladylike risk. There wasn't a doubt in my mind that Grandmother would be receiving a note about my unruly behavior.

Adele watched me closely, her lips puckered into a tight line. I cut my eyes away from her and did a fast scan of the fence. The stranger was gone. Miss Doucette led us all inside and back into the music room. Adele descended upon me as the other girls picked up their instruments.

"You idiot," she hissed lowly, her hands clenched into fists at her sides. "You might have killed yourself climbing down the side of the building. Why didn't you just scream your lungs out until someone rescued you?"

What was this? If not for the hard gleam of her gray eyes and the flare of her dainty nostrils, I might have mistaken her for sounding frightened, or even guilty.

"I don't need rescuing, thank you," I replied. "Did you really think being locked in an old, spooky attic would turn me into a useless ninny?"

I made a show of distraction as I set my recovered music book on the stand. I tried not to let the shake of my hand be noticeable. Adele didn't reply. Each second of silence felt like a strike of victory.

Finally, she spoke. "So you climbed out the window to prove how brave you are?"

I picked up my flute, my palms no longer sweaty with nerves, and met Adele's squinty glare. "I don't need to prove anything to anyone."

She reached past me and shut my music book with a thud. "Except you do, of course. To your uncle. To *Will James.*"

I fumbled with the flute and it fell into my lap.

Adele saw my confusion and reveled in it. But before she or I had a chance to say anything else, Miss Doucette tapped her baton on the music stand before her.

"Flutes first," she said, with a sharp glance my way.

Terrific.

• • •

The hand on the clock clunked down to half past three. The sound echoed through the empty foyer, where I sat on a cushioned bench waiting for my grandmother's carriage. She was fifteen minutes late. I tapped my foot, anxious to be gone from Miss Lydia Doucette's snooty academy — and never return. I was more than ready to go back to the brownstone and demand Grandmother enroll me somewhere else. Or better yet, hire a tutor. But then, I did want to figure out Adele's puzzling mention of Will and Uncle Bruce.

Why would she assume I wanted to prove myself to them? Adele knew all about the Maddie Cook case and had most definitely heard of my uncle. Had she read about Will in the papers, too? The way she'd said Will's name made me wonder if she knew him. If she did, I wanted to know how.

Miss Doucette had left the foyer before she could notice I was still hanging about. I'd busied myself by chronicling the day's events in my notebook, which I'd left in my cloak pocket. By now I'd scribbled furiously about the stranger who had leaped over the fence in a panic when I'd fallen. And that expression of concern on his narrow, distinguished-looking face . . . I wanted to know who he was.

The door to the dining room swung open, and the kitchen girl who'd served us lunch exited with a tea tray. She eyed me suspiciously as she hurried by and up the stairs, no doubt to deliver tea to Miss Doucette. She might very well deliver the news that a girl hadn't been claimed just yet.

"Come on," I whispered with another glance at the clock. The tempo of my foot increased against the shiny parquet floor.

The minute hand jumped another notch. *That's it.* I shot off the bench and threw on my cloak. The brownstone was only a few blocks away. I'd climbed down a fire escape already today. Walking home couldn't be *that* difficult.

Outside, a bracing wind tousled my braids, loosening the plaits Grandmother's industrious servant, Bertie, had created that morning. The wind blew back my cloak. I gathered it around me and headed toward the next street ahead.

"Zanna!" a voice called out from behind me.

I spun around and saw Will James waving from the academy steps. He jogged toward me.

"Will!" I wasn't able to contain my smile. He was wearing a school uniform of his own, but he'd been spared the ridiculous plaid pattern Miss Doucette had settled on.

Will nicked off his hat to greet me. "I was hoping to catch you before you went home. Your grandmother sent over a note saying you'd arrived. How are you, Zanna? Liking Boston?"

Will's blond hair blew about, and his creamy cheeks were flushed. He'd apprenticed with Uncle Bruce last summer. At first it had made me burn with jealousy. Being a detective and apprenticing with Uncle Bruce had been my dream for years. But now I liked Will too much to be envious.

"I could do without Miss Lydia Doucette's Academy,"

I answered, winning a laugh from Will, "but otherwise, it's great. My grandmother seems wonderful. Uncle Bruce seems . . . himself."

Will smiled and put his hat back on. "Yeah, he was happy to be rid of me when Bellmont's started back up. It's a boys' academy."

The wind pushed up the brim of Will's hat. He clapped a hand on top to keep it from blowing away.

"Are you walking home?" he asked, frowning.

"I was going to attempt not getting lost," I answered with a shrug. "Grandmother never sent the carriage."

I tried to laugh, but it was still embarrassing. Will gestured to the sidewalk before us.

"Knight Street is just a little bit from here. Come on," he said, and we started walking. "Listen, I know I'm at school and Uncle Bruce has washed his hands of me, but I'm still following the case he and Detective Grogan are working on." I immediately took out my notebook. He saw it and shook his head, laughing. "I've got to get one of those."

We started walking up the next block.

"The Horne fires?" I asked.

"You know of them already?" He whistled and looked sideways at me. "I knew your coming would be a good thing."

At the cross street, Will led me to the left. I slowed my pace, suddenly not in any hurry to get to Knight Street.

"There've been a few arsons along the harbor front over the last month. Uncle Bruce is focusing the investigation on some Irish crime ringleaders." Will stopped and looked at me sideways. "So you really don't like Miss Doucette's?"

I paused my pencil, confused. "What does that have to do with the fires?"

"Well, don't be angry, but I kind of suggested your grandmother enroll you there. I wanted you to meet Adele Horne."

Adele *Horne*?

"Oh. I met her, all right." So that was how she knew Will — the investigation.

Will started walking again and I tried to write and walk without tripping.

"Xavier Horne is Adele's dad. He's a big grocery supplier and owns the two warehouses that have been burned. The first fire happened before Bellmont's started back up, so I got to work on it with Uncle Bruce. But you know how he is," Will said with a sour tone that I fully understood. "He didn't want me in the way, so I hung around with Adele. After the second fire, she sent me a note, saying she had a theory. And it was pretty interesting."

I didn't particularly like that Adele had a theory Will thought was interesting. I'd rather he tell me how much he couldn't stand her.

"What kind of theory?" I asked anyway.

We came to Bishop Street and Will led me down it, neither of us hurrying now.

"Uncle Bruce and Detective Grogan are investigating these fires as arsons. They think whoever is setting the fires is trying to destroy Mr. Horne's businesses — the primary suspects so far have been associated with the local Irish mob. Mr. Horne is already at odds with them. He's been pretty outspoken against some of their leaders."

I didn't know any of the details regarding the fires, but that theory sounded reasonable and solid enough to me.

"And what does Adele think?" I asked.

Another sign announced we'd reached Grandmother's block. Will's eyes rested on 224 Knight Street four houses down on the left before answering.

"That instead of investigating arson, the police should be investigating art theft."

I didn't know what I'd been expecting, but it

definitely had not been art theft. The idea was so surprising that I couldn't even mock it properly.

"Art theft?" I echoed. "But what would lead her to think that?"

"Not what. *Who,*" Will replied. I stared at him blankly until he realized he needed to explain further. "Listen, Mr. Horne is known around Boston as this big art collector — paintings, sculptures, whatever he can get his hands on. He's got so much, he can't keep it all inside his own house over on June Street. So Adele tells me he secretly stores the art in safes hidden inside his warehouses. He switches around the pieces that are on display in his house a few times a year so everything he has gets the chance to be put on show. The ones not on show go back to the warehouses."

I wrote everything down feverishly. My hand began to cramp. "So *who* led Adele to believe her father's art was being stolen instead of burned?"

Will courteously waited to begin until I'd stopped scribbling. "I wasn't at the second warehouse fire scene, but Adele was. She said some man — someone she'd never met before — told her the art wasn't being destroyed like everyone thought. That it was being nicked right out from under everyone's noses."

Adele trusted some random stranger's opinion versus that of Bruce Snow, a successful and seasoned detective? I arched an eyebrow to show Will what I thought of *that*.

He held up his hand, palm out as if to fend off my skepticism. "I know exactly what you're thinking."

"'That there are more holes in Adele's theory than a slice of Swiss cheese?"

Will laughed. "I know it sounds far-fetched. But after the first two fires, Mr. Horne decided to move the rest of his art from the remaining two warehouses to other locations, a few private homes. Any guesses as to what happened next?"

I didn't particularly enjoy baited questions, but there was no way around this one. "More fires?"

"No. One of the homes was burglarized, and the paintings Mr. Horne stored there were stolen."

I had to admit that was a bit curious. "What happened to the rest of the art he moved from the warehouses?"

Will's shoulders rose up to his ears in an animated shrug. "I guess it's safe so far. I haven't heard anything from Adele and there haven't been any more fires."

I tapped my pencil against the page. "Mr. Horne didn't take his art to a bank vault. Why?"

Will nodded, seeming happy I'd asked. "Because he doesn't trust the banks. There's no proof of anything, of course, but you never know who's tied to the mob.

And since the mob and Mr. Horne aren't friendly, well, you can see why he only trusts himself."

Another minute pondering Adele's surprising theory turned up yet another sizable hole in it.

"Were the safes destroyed in the fires?" I asked. My father's safe at the Rosemount was solid steel. Fire wouldn't eat through that.

"They were made from steel and wood," Will answered. "So the remains were burned-out steel shells with some unidentifiable rubble inside."

Which Mr. Horne and the police assumed was the destroyed artworks.

"I'm guessing Uncle Bruce didn't take Adele's theory seriously?" I asked. According to my uncle, children weren't reliable witnesses. It had to do with too-active imaginations and underdeveloped occipital lobes, or so he said. Personally, I just thought Uncle Bruce disliked children in general.

Will's smug expression faltered. "Do you even need to ask?" His lips pursed and twisted to one side. "I don't even know if I totally believe it. But Adele's nice and she asked me for help. We won't be able to see each other as much since we're at different schools, so I thought you two might be able to check things out together. Kind of like how we worked together in Loch Harbor?"

My mind stuck to the *"Adele's nice"* comment. I must have made an appalled expression, because Will frowned and shifted to the side, looking uneasy.

"She's *nice*? I don't think so, Will," I said. "She locked me in the attic at Miss Doucette's!"

Will stopped and dropped his jaw. *"What?"*

I closed my notebook and shoved it deep into my cloak pocket. "She can't possibly want my help. Besides, her whole theory is a mess: She's basing everything on what some random stranger told her. She has no proof for any of it."

Warehouses burned down to cover the tracks of a true crime of art theft . . . it was too flimsy. Too extreme. And it was exactly the kind of thing that got my blood pumping fast and hot.

Will took a few slow steps toward Grandmother's house without a reply. I felt bad for taking out my frustration on him, but how could he actually like Adele? After the stunt she pulled that afternoon, I wouldn't help tie her shoelace, let alone solve the art thefts or arsons or whatever they really were.

"I have to go. I'm sure my grandmother will be wondering where I am," I said, but then remembered that she'd forgotten to send a carriage for me in the first place.

"Sure," Will said. "But will you at least think about

talking to Adele? I don't know why she'd lock you in some attic. . . . Maybe if you tell her you saw me, she'll know that I told you everything, and that she can trust you. Okay?"

I muttered a weak promise that I would and then said a hasty good-bye, rushing down the street toward the brownstone. Talk to Adele? I dreaded even seeing her the next day.

I reached the front steps to Grandmother's home, still fuming. I opened the door and came face-to-face with a tall man with a crisp black hat and a long black overcoat. I screamed, and the man shot out his hand and slapped it over my mouth.

Chapter Four

• • •

Detective Rule: Real detectives do not scream. They may flinch or startle, but they do not scream. Ever.

• • •

THE MAN DROPPED HIS SWEATY PALM FROM my mouth and grimaced. "Great heavens, child!"

My blanched face started to color again as embarrassment settled in. This man didn't have the narrow, defined cheekbones that the stranger at the academy had. The man standing in Grandmother's foyer was about fifty pounds heavier, too, with bristly white eyebrows overdue for a good trim.

"Who are you?" I asked. He puckered up his lips.

"Who am I? *I* am Dr. Philbrick, young lady."

Doctor? "Has something happened? Is my grandmother sick?"

I tried to rush past him, but Dr. Philbrick held his black leather doctor's bag up in my path.

"Your grandmother is resting at the moment, and is not to be disturbed."

"I want to know what's happened." I lifted my chin and attempted to look indomitable.

He huffed with impatience, but his arm couldn't hold up the bulky leather bag any longer and it flopped to his side in defeat.

"Your grandmother has had one of her attacks." Dr. Philbrick sounded put out by having to speak to me.

"An attack? What kind of attack?"

Attack was such a brutal word. It made me think of strangulation and bloody hammerheads and all sorts of terrible things normal girls my age probably never thought about.

"An attack of the nervous system," the doctor answered.

I sighed in relief, which only seemed to irritate him further.

"It's quite serious for a woman of her age and constitution, I assure you." He pushed back his shoulders and sniffed. "Mrs. Snow hasn't suffered from one of these attacks for quite some time. When she has one, it hinders her ability to breathe."

I suddenly felt guilty. Here I'd thought she'd simply forgotten to send the carriage for me — even got aggravated with her for it — and she'd been having an attack the whole time.

"I take it you are her visiting granddaughter?" Dr. Philbrick didn't wait for an answer. "The servants have been instructed on the dosage of the tonic and powders that I've left. As to helping Mrs. Snow win back her health, I suggest you give her nothing to worry about. Nothing at all. Stress induces the attacks." He scoffed at me. "I wouldn't be surprised if your arrival is the very thing that brought on this episode."

Bertie, the serving girl, appeared around the twist in the stairwell right at that moment, saving me from acting out on my impulse to kick Dr. Philbrick in the shin.

"Oh, Miss Zanna! You've arrived, thank goodness. Mrs. Snow is asking for you." Bertie's voice had the sweet, high pitch of a songbird.

The doctor lifted both of his bushy brows. "No. Stress." He opened the front door and left without another remark.

I went straight to the stairs without taking off my cloak. "That man is wretched!"

Bertie nodded, leading the way. "That he is. But he's Lawton Square's best physician. We called for him straightaway when we realized the mistress was having an episode. She hasn't had one in so long. . . ."

I wanted to ask how long had been "so long," but Bertie was shuffling too fast down the hallway. Electric

49

light poured out of each frosted-glass sconce mounted on the papered walls every few feet. Bertie rapped pertly on the door to Grandmother's room, waited until the count of three, and then opened it.

"Mrs. Snow, your granddaughter," Bertie announced. I entered with hesitation. What did one look like after an attack of the nervous system? I half expected Grandmother to be splayed out in her bed like an invalid, her hair a mess around her shoulders, her eyes sunken in and rimmed by dark circles.

But that wasn't the scene that greeted me at all. Grandmother was sitting upright in a regal-looking chair in front of her fireplace. Other than a few silver curls framing her face, her hair was done up into a perfectly knotted bun. Her cheeks were slightly pink, but her ice blue eyes were just as bright and clear as ever.

"Zanna, darling, come in and sit with me." She gestured to the matching chair beside her. I crossed the carpeted floor to her side.

"Oh, Grandmother, the doctor told me about the attack, and how you'd stopped breathing." I took her hand and felt its dry warmth.

"Jeremiah Philbrick exaggerates," Grandmother said with a wry grin. "If he had his way, I'd never do anything but sit in this chair and watch the logs in the fireplace burn and crumble."

She let go of my hand and I sat opposite her. "He and Bertie said you haven't had one of these attacks lately." I watched Grandmother play with the colored glass beads on her necklace. "Do you think that it's because . . . because I've come here to live with you? That it's too much stress?'"

I thought I saw her hand tremble, but she returned it to her lap too soon to be sure.

"Heavens, no! Why, you silly goose, you're no stress at all, so put that out of your head! No, today . . . well, today I exerted myself by helping Margaret Mary with the silver, among other preparations. She can cook a roast to perfection, but give her a cloth and polish and she's useless."

I'd met the Irish cook that morning at breakfast. She looked like she'd cooked — and sampled — plenty of perfect roasts in her lifetime, and her eggs and bacon and poached pear rivaled Nellie's.

"You worked yourself up over tarnished silverware?" I asked.

Grandmother took out a lace hankie from up her sleeve and shook it at me.

"Of course! I can't have our dinner guests on Saturday sit down to eat and pick up a spotty spoon or blackened fork. I'd be mortified!"

"You didn't say anything about a dinner party," I

said, though dinner itself did sound very tempting right then. I'd hardly had a bite of the meal served at school.

"How else am I to introduce my granddaughter to Lawton Square society? After the dinner party, I'm sure we'll receive enough invitations to salons and parties to last you through your stay," Grandmother said. I could tell this made her happy, and not at all stressed.

I indulged her with a wide smile while clenching my teeth in fear. Grandmother would expect me to be social, and proper, and . . . and . . . a *lady*. I was undoubtedly going to disappoint her. And that, of course, would bring on stress.

"That sounds wonderful!" I said, though the gusto was a bit extreme.

Grandmother didn't notice. Her train of thought switched tracks and her contented smile was replaced by a look of horror.

"Oh, the florist!" she cried. "I completely forgot, he's coming to see what arrangements will suit the rooms for this Saturday. I must remind Bertie."

She started to lift herself from her chair. I leaped up. "No, let me. I'll tell Bertie."

Grandmother wobbled and it didn't take much of a nudge to guide her back to her seat. She ran a delicate hand over her eyes, rubbing them slightly. "Perhaps you're right, darling. Yes, you can remind Bertie."

I started for the door.

"Oh, and, Zanna, can you . . ." She cleared her throat with a few dainty coughs. "Can you ask Margaret Mary to bring me Dr. Philbrick's powders?"

It seemed to pain her to admit to needing them. My father had a stubborn streak, too, and seeing Grandmother's made me miss him. But I wouldn't have time for homesickness now, not with a finishing school to fear, dinner parties to attend, and my dreaded assignment from Will to speak to Adele about the Horne fires.

● ● ●

By the third day of school, I still hadn't found the strength to speak to Adele about the fires or her art theft theory. It seemed the more the other girls surrounded and badgered me with questions about Maddie's case and my uncle Bruce, the more withdrawn and cold Adele became. Every time she speared me with one of her foul glares, I remembered her wicked laughter through the attic door right after she'd locked me inside. It never failed to make me steam.

On the fourth day, Miss Doucette decided to take the fourteen of us to the Boston Public Garden for a morning of sketching. It was a warm day, a holdover from the summer, the sun bright and the sky clear. We sat on stools spread out among the maze of paths through dying late-summer blooms.

I heard the buzz of a bee circling my head as I stared at the barely touched sketch pad in front of me. The sun reflected off the paper, my sharpened graphite pencil useless in my fingers. Unless it was a magical pencil, infused with powers of creating fine art, I was doomed. Instead, I longed to take my notebook out of my cloak pocket and jot down character sketches on all of the girls.

Two rows of withering cattails away, I saw Adele beneath the drooping branches of a crab apple tree. She concentrated on her sketch, her hand moving deftly over her paper. I looked at the few unformed lines on my paper. A two-year-old could do better. If I had to show my sketch of a sunflower to the rest of the girls, I might just keel over with an acute attack of humiliationitis.

Adele glanced up from her drawing and met my panicked eyes. She rose from her stool and wandered along the brick path, continuing to sketch as she walked. I bit the inside of my bottom lip. Adele was walking right toward me. Perfect. What would she do now?

She stopped at a fork in the garden path and took a fast, discreet look around. I knew that move — she was checking to see if anyone had taken notice of her ambling. But from what I'd witnessed the last few days, Adele wasn't close friends with anyone at the academy, and no one took notice of her now. Even Miss Doucette had her back turned as she commented on some other girl's work near a small duck pond.

My interest piqued, I watched Adele as she turned back toward me. Her gray eyes widened and rolled toward the turn in the brick path. Twice. She then slowly started off in that direction. I couldn't believe it. Adele Horne wanted me to follow her. I sat still, suspicious. Following her might only lead me straight into another one of her traps.

But Will would want me to. He would be at Grandmother's dinner on Saturday evening and he'd want to know what Adele had said. If I didn't have anything to share with him, what use would I be? Besides, I couldn't allow Adele the pleasure of knowing she made me nervous.

A bee buzzed near my ear and I shot up from my stool, my jerky movements garnering some attention from Maud and Lucille, two of the girls who'd befriended me — if consistently begging me to introduce them to *the* Detective Bruce Snow could even be seen as real friendship.

I ignored them and attempted to sketch and walk as Adele had, but by the time I reached the bend in the path, my drawing was beyond repair. I flipped the page and sighed lovingly at the blank white sheet. It reminded me of my notebook, and how every new sheet of paper inside had the possibility of one day holding a pivotal clue.

Adele was just a few yards ahead of me, under a short tunnel of arched trellis. Vines had climbed up the sides and woven into the roof to create natural shade from the sun. There were no other students in sight as Adele waved her hand for me to hurry.

"I wondered how long it would take you," she hissed. "We only have a few moments before Miss Doucette notices we've wandered off."

I crossed my arms, my sketch pad tight against my chest. "What, exactly, do you want?"

I took stock of my surroundings, trying to anticipate what Adele could use against me.

"Have you talked to Will yet?" Adele asked.

I quit looking at the thorny vines running up the trellis, having pictured them briefly as a weapon of some kind.

"Yes, I have, and I know all about your interesting theory." Adele narrowed her eyes as she picked up on my sarcasm. "What do I have to do with any of it?"

She drew her shoulders back, hesitating. Without meeting my eyes, Adele answered, lightning quick, "Will said you might be able to help."

She looked a little like Uncle Bruce had when he'd finally admitted I'd done well in the Maddie Cook case: queasy.

"And why would I want to?" I asked. "For some reason, you decided to make my first day at Miss Doucette's a nightmare. And now you're asking for my help?"

Adele hushed me and then craned her neck to see if anyone was coming.

"Trust me — I'd much rather not have to ask. I would love to be able to solve this on my own and not have to bother asking for help from anybody."

I had never met anyone so stubborn in all my life!

"Then why are you?" I asked.

"Because it's not my *father's* art that's being stolen!" Adele's voice was the one rising now, and she didn't check it. "It was my mother's dream to open an art museum, not his. When she died —" Adele swallowed and tried to regain her cool composure.

"When she died, Papa took over the collecting. He wouldn't sell any of her pieces, even when we ran out of room in the house to display them. It's important to him, and I don't want to see any more of it being taken."

I took a breath, not sure what to say. Her mother had died. What do you say to someone whose mother is dead? *I'm sorry* wasn't good enough. I decided to skip over the topic altogether.

"So you believe the art was stolen before the warehouses were burned? Will said that some strange man tipped you off."

Adele exhaled and her tense shoulders dropped in a show of relief.

"It happened at the second warehouse fire. I was standing apart from everyone who was sifting through the wreckage, including Detective Snow."

The mention of my uncle set off a tremor inside me. It spiked my pulse and made my stomach twist. I was partly frustrated with him, but partly proud, too. It didn't make sense.

"This man — I don't know who he was — stepped up beside me and commented what a shame the fire was, how it must have destroyed so many valuable things inside." Adele frowned, shaking her head as she remembered. "I think I said something along the lines of 'You have no idea.' And then the man said the oddest thing: He said that he *did* have an idea. He came right out and said that the art my father had been hiding inside his warehouses had been stolen, not destroyed. Then he told me to tell Detective Snow something even more strange: He wanted me to tell him that the red herrings had returned, but that they were a new breed."

Adele stopped to take a breath and then glanced down at my sketch pad. I realized I had filled in half of the blank page with messy scribbles — everything Adele was telling me.

"A new breed of red herrings?" I asked, intrigued.

"False clues," she said haughtily, as if I didn't already know what a red herring was. "They're used to lead investigations in the wrong direction."

"I *know*."

She glowered. "You would think Detective Snow would have known as well. But when I finally got to him and told him what the stranger had said, he acted as if he had no idea what that meant. He . . . he *humiliated* me. He practically accused me of lying. I'm certain if my father had heard the way he belittled me . . ." Adele sputtered over her words. What would her father have been able to do? Get him kicked off the case? I doubted it.

As much as I didn't like her, I didn't think Adele was lying. "Did my uncle see this stranger?"

Adele shook her head. "By the time I'd fetched Detective Snow, he was gone. And I couldn't give a very good description of him because he'd been wearing a hat low over his eyes, and I — well, he'd been a stranger and I knew I wasn't supposed to talk to him or look him in the eye."

No doubt one of Miss Doucette's rules. It certainly

wasn't a rule of mine. There was only one way for a detective to treat strangers: with thorough observation. A strange man had presented the idea of the art being stolen. He'd known about the pieces being hidden in the warehouses and had decided to share his theory with Adele. But why? Had the man been the thief himself? And the "new breed of red herrings" comment sounded like a code of some sort. A code meant for my uncle to decipher, though it sounded as if he'd overlooked it.

"Can you remember anything about him?" I asked, unsatisfied. "Anything distinguishable at all?"

She'd recalled his words so perfectly. There must be something more.

"He smelled," Adele finally said, though she didn't seem very sure of herself.

"Badly? Of what?" I wrote *odd smell* on the paper.

"No, not badly," she answered, licking her lips as she remembered more. "No, it was more like a soapy smell. But it wasn't flowery or perfumed. It was musky. Like wood."

She shook her head. "Or maybe it was just the burned wood of the warehouse. I don't know. What does it matter? We can't possibly track someone down by the way they smell."

My pencil halted.

"We?"

Adele sighed. "Yes, we. I'm sorry I wasn't nice, but I had to test you out. You understand, don't you? If you'd come down out of that attic weeping like a fool and pointing a finger at me, then I would have known not to put any stock in all the things Will and the papers had said about you. But instead, you climbed out of the highest window and down a fire escape." Adele rolled her eyes, but I could tell she was impressed. I didn't need Adele's approval, but still . . . it was a *little* satisfying.

"Adele? Suzanna?" Miss Doucette rounded the corner of the path and spotted us under the trellis. "Girls, are you sketching in there?"

I flipped to my previous page with the sad excuse for a sunflower.

"Oh, yes, Miss Doucette," Adele said sweetly. "The pattern of the trelliswork is such a challenge."

I stared at her, impressed she'd thought it up off the top of her head. But then she turned her sketch pad outward to show Miss Doucette. She actually *had* sketched the trellis. But when? She hadn't so much as lifted her pencil the whole time we'd been standing there.

"Lovely, Adele. As always." Our teacher beamed. She then peeked at my sketch pad. Her glowing smile dimmed. "Oh. Well. That trellis does seem to be a challenge, doesn't it? Perhaps you should try one of the ferns?"

She extended her arm and we followed her cue to move along. Adele arched her eyebrow again, this time at me. She'd already drawn the trellis before getting up from her stool earlier. She'd covered her tracks, preparing for Miss Doucette's arrival should we be found apart from the group. Her preparedness impressed me more than I would ever dare admit.

Chapter Five

• • •

Sat., Sept. 19, 6 p.m.: Conducting research via newspaper clippings provided by Will.

— Horne fire #1 (Aug. 24) involved a warehouse of cabbage and broccoli. 3 paintings lost.

— Horne fire #2 (Sept. 2) involved a warehouse of canned sardines and kippers. 2 paintings lost.

Possible Theory: Someone is trying to stop the Boston population from consuming fish and vegetables.

• • •

AN HOUR BEFORE GRANDMOTHER'S DINNER guests were to arrive, Bertie came into my room and laid my dress out over the bed's postage-stamp quilt. On top of that, she laid a rectangular envelope: a Western Union telegram.

"It just arrived," Bertie said of the telegram. She didn't need to say who'd sent it. If my parents continued to send the thirty-cent telegrams at the same rate for the next few months, they'd most likely fund the laying of a whole new telegraph cable.

But it wasn't the telegram that held my attention. Bertie stepped back and I stared at the dress — at the navy blue material trimmed in white ribbon, the squared shoulders, and the collar complete with a droopy bow tie.

"It's . . ." I hesitated, heart plunging. "It's a sailor dress."

Bertie coughed politely. "The late Mr. Snow was an admiral in the navy."

I glanced up from the disappointing dress. "He was?"

The corner of Bertie's mouth turned downward. "You didn't know?"

I ran my fingers over the stiff shoulder pads of the much-too-childish sailor dress, and then picked up the telegram. My father had sent this one, the shortened, economical sentences asking after my health and schooling.

"No, I didn't know." My father never really talked about Boston or his family. All my parents had ever said was that Boston just hadn't been for them. They'd wanted a slower life. A quieter life.

"Do you need help dressing, Miss Zanna?" Bertie asked.

"I can manage." I had no desire to share the moment of humiliation when I put on the dress.

Bertie gave a pert nod and left the room. Eyeing the sailor dress, I knew I had no choice. I had to wear it. And the moment of humiliation arrived just as I'd predicted.

I came off the last step of the stairwell, my sweaty hand gripping the carved mahogany wood of the newel post, and met with a full receiving room of men and women. Each and every one of them stopped to turn and welcome me. Grandmother threw up her arms and squealed like she had just seen the world's most adorable baby.

"Oh! Look at that!" She cut a path through all of her guests and gripped me by my mortarboard shoulders. "Oh, this dress! It would have made my dear Roger so very proud."

Mortified, I tried to avoid the crush of eyes inspecting my ridiculous dress as murmurs of agreement sounded. I noted instead how the furniture in the receiving room — the grand room parallel to Grandmother's cluttered parlor — had all been pushed up against the walls. Everyone milled about on the checkered parquet floor, tall glasses of champagne in their hands, while wreathes of cigar and pipe smoke hovered overhead in the soft lighting from suspended candelabras. It reminded me of a miniature version of the Rosemount's Great Hall.

Grandmother finally let go of my shoulders and thrust me into the center of the crowd. "Go on now, Zanna dear, and don't be shy." She winked one of her bright, cerulean eyes at me. "I believe a friend of yours is here, too."

I finally lifted my face to scan the crowd. A friend? Will? I heard the rumble of Uncle Bruce's laugh somewhere deeper within the receiving room. I craned my neck and refused to stand still long enough for anyone to catch my attention and witness firsthand my less-than-appealing social skills.

The tail of the floppy navy blue ribbon holding back my hair swung in front of my eyes and tickled my nose. I swatted it away, and while doing so, I bumped shoulders with someone.

"Pardon me," I said quickly, and started to take off once again.

"Some sailor you'd be. You can't even navigate your way through a party."

The soles of my buckled leather dress shoes skidded to a stop. I turned around, and with mounting despair, saw a head of silky black curls offset by snowy cheeks, pouting lips, and an arched eyebrow.

"Adele?" I hadn't known she would be coming.

I took in her lovely pale green silk dress, the single row of creamy white ruffles along the hem, and the soft billows of silk around her shoulders. What on earth was Adele Horne doing at my grandmother's dinner? And why did she have to be wearing the most beautiful dress I'd ever seen?

I forced the thought away and remembered something I'd wanted to ask her. "Listen, I'm glad you're here," I began.

She looked sideways at me. "You are?"

After the mild case of frostbite I'd suffered from Adele's cold shoulder all week, I supposed my claim did seem suspicious. But this was business.

"I've been trying to form a time line of events, and wanted to know when your father moved the rest of his art from the warehouses to the other locations."

Adele ran a few fingers through her curls absent-mindedly. "After the second fire on September —"

"September second." I already knew it. *The second on the second* was how I'd memorized it.

She quit playing with her hair and clasped her hands behind her back. "I didn't need reminding, Suzanna. The second fire on the second of September."

My posture wilted, not pleased at all that someone else had used my method of memorization.

"Did he move the art from the other warehouses that same day?" I asked.

She shook her head, glancing around the crowded room. We were shorter than most of the adults, and hence easily overlooked. Sometimes that came in handy.

"No, the next day," she answered.

I needed my notebook. Unfortunately, the sailor dress lacked pockets.

"And where were these other locations?" I asked. But Adele wasn't able to answer. Just then, a short, compact man with a handlebar mustache approached us.

"Well, Midge, who do you have here?" the man asked. He wrapped his arm around Adele's shoulders.

"*Papa*," she groaned. He squeezed her tightly and laughed. ·

"Oh, that's right." He leaned in closer to me and, with a conspiratorial whisper, said, "I forgot I'm not supposed to call her that in public."

Midge? I reveled in Adele's inflamed cheeks and pursed lips. Mr. Horne straightened back up and raised his voice to its normal tenor.

"But certainly there isn't any harm if your friend here knows your pet name."

Adele's scowl deepened.

"I'm Xavier Horne, and you must be the guest of honor, Suzanna."

He held out his hand. I took it, preparing to shake. But he kissed the back of my hand instead, his mustache whiskers tickling my skin.

"*Enchanté, mademoiselle*," he said.

From what little French I knew, I replied, "*Merci*."

He said something else in French but I didn't understand. He must have noticed my confusion, because he laughed again. His eyes were the same light gray as Adele's, but they were merry. Adele's were flinty and apprehensive, as if she never found anything humorous or likable at all. I observed the rest of his characteristics and planned to add them later to his profile in my notebook.

Xavier Horne was just an inch taller than his daughter, who stood a full head taller than me. He wore an expensive-looking suit with a gold chain drooped over his vest, indicating a pocket watch in his left chest pocket. He sparkled from his balding head to his cuff links. The tips of his black dress shoes were the only things out of place. They were both lightly dusted with a gray sort of substance. It looked like ash. I wondered why he hadn't bothered to wipe them off before tonight's dinner.

"Xavier, there you are." Uncle Bruce's voice came up behind me. He wore a crisp black suit and tie, and as always, he dwarfed those around him with his height, his voice, and his presence. "I had hoped you would be joining Neil and me at the club tonight before the dinner party."

Xavier Horne patted my uncle on the shoulder. "Sorry to miss it. I had some business to attend to. Came here straight after."

I took another covert glance at his shoes. Whatever sort of business he'd been seeing to must have involved getting ash on his dress shoes, and he hadn't had time to polish them up before dinner.

"I'm glad to see you now, at least," Uncle Bruce continued, a short tumbler filled with crushed ice and a fizzy liquid in his hand. "We've got one of your dockworkers claiming —"

Xavier Horne held his hand up. "No, not another word, Detective."

Uncle Bruce lowered his drink. "Excuse me?"

He clearly didn't like being interrupted. He flicked his eyes toward me but only for a millisecond.

"I don't want to discuss the case tonight," Adele's father explained. "I'm here to escape. To relax and welcome your niece to Boston."

Uncle Bruce wriggled his mustache the way he did when bothered.

Mr. Horne turned back toward me. "I am told, Suzanna, if I want true relaxation that Loch Harbor is the place to seek out, is that correct? Your father owns a hotel there?"

"My father and mother manage the Rosemount, but Mr. Blythe in London owns it —"

Mr. Horne's crunched-up eyebrows startled me into silence. "Blythe? Marcus Blythe?"

I nodded.

"Wonderful man, that Marcus Blythe! He's got an impressive hotel right here in Boston, too — the Sherwood. I saw the most gorgeous Cassatt there last spring, but it wasn't for sale."

I saw the opening and lunged for it. "You're fond of art?"

Adele lifted her chin, eyes rounded with surprise. She knew my game.

"Quite," he answered, seemingly delighted by my interest. "I have over two hundred pieces in my personal collection. Cassatt, Monet, Sargent, Manet, Peale, Delacroix . . . paintings, sculpture, illuminated texts, mosaics, glass. Anything that is beautiful to look at, really."

71

I strived to memorize everything but thought I might just have to ask Adele for the artists' names later.

"Your collection must be worth a fortune," I said, hoping my age and mock wonder (*breathless* wonder, at that) made up for how rude it was to mention money.

Mr. Horne didn't seem offended, though. In fact, he puffed out his chest and proudly agreed. "Quite, quite."

"Are any of the pieces insured?" Now that *did* attract a curious glower from my uncle's direction. I scrambled to remedy the blunder. "The Rosemount once had a . . . a sculpture stolen and it wasn't insured. It was devastating."

It wasn't entirely untrue. Old Forrest Johnston, one of the Rosemount's long-standing summer guests, had sculpted a mermaid statue for the hotel and placed a key to his hidden fortune inside. The sculpture had been stolen and destroyed by Maddie Cook's brother, but really the only person who'd been devastated was Mr. Johnston. The statue had been ugly, and I doubted anyone would miss it.

Mr. Horne grumbled in dismay. "All of my pieces are insured, but for a true collector, mere money could never replace the value of a stolen work of art. I've lost many lovely pieces lately, Suzanna — as I'm sure you've heard. They were dear to me, though not just because of what they were worth."

Will and Detective Grogan had stepped into our conversation as Mr. Horne was speaking. I was relieved to see Will. Maybe he could think of some other, less obvious questions to get Mr. Horne to talk more about his art collection.

"Certainly, the insurance money could be used to purchase other works?" Detective Grogan asked. Mr. Horne made a face that resembled mine when my mother insisted I eat every last Brussels sprout on my plate.

"Each piece is one of a kind. Irreplaceable. And every collector has a favorite piece. A crown jewel. If it were to be taken or destroyed . . . like Suzanna said, it would be devastating."

Detective Grogan inspected me from behind his wire-framed eyeglasses. While Uncle Bruce's nature was robust and forceful, his partner's was keen and contemplative.

"But I don't want to discuss the fires tonight," Mr. Horne said again, and with finality. "Suzanna, does the Rosemount have any interesting pieces?"

I frowned. "Not unless you consider taxidermy an art."

"Or deer-antler coatracks," Will added with a laugh. They *were* hard to forget.

Uncle Bruce cracked a grin as he sipped his seltzer water. "I doubt even the crooks running the underground market would consider the décor at the Rosemount worthy of being stolen."

I wasn't a fan of rustic décor, or the stuffed and mounted wildlife hanging around the Great Hall, but Uncle Bruce's insult burned nonetheless.

"Is that where stolen art gets sold, then?" Will asked boldly. "In the underground market?"

Detective Grogan shifted his keen gaze from me to Adele to Will, no doubt connecting our pointed questions to her previously dismissed art theft theory. "Stolen art does, yes. We're watching for any activity regarding the pieces taken in the burglary the day after Xavier had them moved from the warehouse safes."

Detective Grogan paused and studied Mr. Horne a moment. I thought I saw a flicker of mistrust behind those wire-rimmed eyeglasses before he continued. "However, Boston's underground market for art has been quiet these last thirteen years since the end of the Red Herring Heists."

I snapped to attention. Uncle Bruce suddenly gurgled and choked on his drink. Mr. Horne whacked him on the back.

"Slow down, friend," Mr. Horne said. "What you need is a smooth brandy. That blasted seltzer gets me every time."

Uncle Bruce muttered something about a tickle in his throat as Grandmother appeared at my side. I should have said hello, but I could think only of the Red Herring Heists that Detective Grogan had mentioned. It was the second mention of red herrings in one week.

"Neil Grogan, are you discussing work during one of my dinner parties?" Grandmother asked, holding herself in her regal, peacock-like pose. "For shame, young man. I won't have any of it. Now, Xavier, I take it you've met my granddaughter?"

As Grandmother and Mr. Horne exchanged overly complimentary words regarding me, I looked to see Adele's reaction to Grogan's comment. But the black expression she gave me only pointed to how upset she was that her art theft theory was still being dismissed.

"So Miss Suzanna Snow is here for the autumn," Mr. Horne said, dragging me back into the conversation. "Tell me, does your middle name also begin with the letter *S*? My late wife's name was Harriet Hortensia. Can you imagine? Harriet Hortensia Horne!"

Adele wrapped her arms tightly across her waist at the mention of her mother. Her father spoke of her so easily, and yet it was obvious Adele was made uncomfortable by it. He didn't seem to even notice Adele's unease.

"No, my middle name begins with an *L*," I answered. "It stands for —"

"Was that the dinner bell?" Grandmother jumped and twisted around, straining to see through the crowds in her receiving room. At the same instant, Uncle Bruce broke into another fit of coughing and throat clearing.

"Blasted tickle again. I think I do need that brandy after all, Xavier. It looks like you're nearly finished with yours. Why don't we hunt down that decanter before sitting down to eat."

"I didn't hear the bell," I said, certain I wouldn't have missed it. I was positively starving. And Mr. Horne's glass wasn't anywhere near empty.

"I didn't hear it either. How could we above all this din?" Mr. Horne said with a laugh. "But I'm sure Midge is famished. You're always hungry, aren't you, Midge?"

Adele glared at her father, mortified. Though I'd failed to memorize all of the social etiquette rules my mother had tried to teach me, I was pretty sure it was in bad form to mention a lady's voracious appetite.

"As I was saying," I said loudly, trying to distract the awkward silence following Mr. Horne's blunder. "My middle name starts with an *L* and it stands for —"

"Lynne?" Uncle Bruce guessed, interrupting me. He sounded so enthusiastic, too.

"No, not, uh, Lynne..." I stammered with my reply, wondering why he'd have ventured a guess. Surely he didn't care what my middle name was.

"I'm positive I heard that dinner bell," Grandmother said again. The rouge she wore couldn't hide the way her cheeks had quickly paled. "And it's about time!" She clapped her hands together to bring everyone in the room to attention. The chatter dimmed.

"Please, let's proceed to the dining room, shall we?"

Grandmother ushered me along. I tried to say goodbye to Will, Adele, and her father, but Grandmother only shooed me onward more firmly.

"As guest of honor, you'll be seated first, of course," she said. I glanced over my shoulder and saw Uncle Bruce, his cheeks red and nostrils flared.

I faced forward and wondered what it could possibly have to do with my middle name.

Chapter Six

• • •

Sun., Sept. 20.: Things to do:
— Research Boston's underground market
— Research Red Herring Heists
— Learn how to embroider a lace hankie
— Curse Miss Doucette for the rest of eternity

• • •

THERE WERE MANY THINGS I WAS BEGINNING to like about my grandmother. For one, she hadn't yet scolded me for any of the numerous social blunders I'd made at the dinner party the night before (I'd tripped on the leg of a dining room chair; yawned while one of the female guests tediously described the cut, clarity, and carat weight of her diamond necklace; and repeatedly observed the dangerously off-center toupee worn by a guest across the dinner table).

Secondly, Grandmother didn't make polite talk. After spending every summer surrounded by polite, pleasant people at the overly proper Rosemount, it was refreshing to be with someone who didn't hesitate to cut another person to the quick.

As I hid behind a statue of Adonis inside the Bentworth Museum courtyard, working in my notebook, Grandmother sneaked up beside me and proved I wasn't safe from her biting words either.

"Zanna, put that blasted thing away! What are you scribbling about this time? We're going to be late for the concert."

Grandmother had left my side five minutes before to speak with an old friend by the topiary, and I'd decided to use the time wisely. There was just too much to do, and as I kept up with Grandmother's rushed stroll along the museum's brick path, I wished I hadn't had to come to this concert. But *Music is culture, and culture is what feeds our souls*, as Grandmother recited twice on the carriage ride there.

The practicing strings of a violin trio dripped through the twilight as we left the open-roofed courtyard, which was at the center of the museum and surrounded on all sides by four floors of arabesque windows and walkways. Lights flickered throughout the garden area and glowed through the museum's foreign-looking windows.

"Last night's dinner party was nice," I said to her as we followed a queue of other concertgoers inside.

Grandmother had been oddly silent all day. Ever since declaring she'd heard the dinner bell chiming, she'd been acting frazzled and out of sorts. All of the guests had streamed into the dining room, and just as I'd suspected, the waiters had not been there to seat us. The water goblets were empty, the champagne bottles still corked. Dinner had not been ready after all, but Grandmother hadn't cared. She'd directed us to our seats herself until the waiters heard us from the kitchen and rushed in, alarmed and spouting off apologies.

"Yes, darling, I'm happy you enjoyed yourself."

I waited for her to say more . . . perhaps something about how "charming" my horrid sailor's dress had been, or the gleaming china, or the salmon pâté to which Margaret Mary had added too much paprika. Nothing.

"I did. It was nice to meet Adele's father. She and Mr. Horne are very . . . different from each other."

Grandmother flicked her wrist as we sped through a doorway. Her silk fan snapped open and she began fanning herself as our line of coiffed, cologned, and perfumed ladies and men climbed a spiral stone staircase.

"Detective Grogan brought up an interesting topic, too. He mentioned a case from about thirteen years ago called the Red Herring Heists. Do you remember them?" I asked.

We'd reached the top of the stairs, and Grandmother had started to breathe heavily. Now she stumbled to the side, as though her knees had given way. I grasped her arm and tried to hold her steady.

"Grandmother? Are you not feeling well enough for the concert?"

She started her fan back up. "I think we should go inside and find a seat."

We followed the others to the second-floor hall. The trio had finished warming up and was waiting to begin properly. Seats had been arranged throughout a large room, where the walls were hung with paintings. Lush potted shrubbery had been arranged in every corner, along with randomly scattered sculpture. Grandmother found her way toward the front of the room, close to the players, and chose two seats in the center of a row. I sat beside her and noticed a sheen of perspiration on her forehead and nose.

"We should leave," I whispered as the chatter started to dim. "You're not well."

She shook her head and waved off my concern. Dr. Philbrick had said stress brought on her breathing attacks. I'd only asked about the Red Herring Heists. I considered how that could be stressful. Was there something about the old case that bothered Grandmother?

The trio began, the first sharp notes of the piece so startling and quick that I jumped in my seat. The playing immediately slowed, taking on a more soothing, soft rhythm, and my heartbeat returned to normal. I felt silly and looked to see if anyone had noticed. Everyone seemed to be concentrating solely on the musicians, who were all dressed in crisp black suits, their hair glossed back.

Grandmother laid a hand on my arm. I could feel the dampness of her palm, even through her white silk gloves.

"I'm going to the back windows for some fresh air," she whispered into my ear. I moved to get up with her, but her grip on my arm tightened. "No, stay and enjoy the music, Zanna. I'll be fine by myself for a few minutes."

She rose from her chair and disappeared behind the seated guests without drawing a single curious or annoyed glance. I followed her with my eyes until I was turning in my seat and inviting attention from the row behind me. I faced forward again, uneasy.

The string music slid between fast tempos and heated whines, to velvet sighs, so light and airy they could have easily lulled me to sleep. A minute slipped by, then two, and then I lost count. I only knew that Grandmother had been gone longer than I'd expected.

Another minute ticked by, the empty chair beside me growing louder than the violins echoing through the gallery hall. I finally got to my feet and, as swiftly as possible, headed for the back of the room, toward the windows that overlooked the courtyard. Grandmother wasn't standing near any of them. To my relief, she wasn't sprawled out on the floor, either.

But then I saw her. I rested my hand on the casement of an open window in the back of the music hall, and through one of the curved arabesque windows in an adjacent hallway I saw Grandmother's swept-up gray curls. Her head was turned, showing only her profile. She was speaking, it seemed, though the person she addressed was not visible.

A nearby door led to the hallway in which she stood. I went and peeked around the corner. New moonlight streamed in through the open-roofed courtyard and lit the corridor, along with a few flickering lanterns of candlelight. The violinists were playing their instruments so loudly, nothing Grandmother said to the person, who was cloaked in shadow, was able to reach my ears. Perhaps it was only Uncle Bruce, or Mr. Horne. But the clandestine meeting gave off too strong a mysterious undertone.

I stayed where I was, peering around the corner as the trio lowered the pitch and fever of their music. I finally heard a portion of what Grandmother was saying.

". . . doesn't matter. You cannot be here."

"I'm sorry if my following you tonight has upset you, Octavia, but I have every right to be here. I thought, if anyone, *you* might understand." The person in the shadows was a man, and his voice was raspy but articulate. And firm. It was a familiar voice, but I couldn't place why, or to whom it belonged.

I crept closer, hiding behind a leafy potted plant.

"You thought I might understand? What involving you could I ever understand? It's because of you that my son ... that he ..." Grandmother choked on her words, raising a closed fist to her lips. "It's all your doing!"

The man started to say something else, but Grandmother wavered and collapsed onto the floor in a heap of taffeta and lace. Her head knocked the stone with an audible *crack*.

"Grandmother!" I shouted just as the music jumped yet again into a sharp, furious tempo.

I raced out from behind the potted shrubbery and to her side. The man she'd been talking to knelt down as well. I shook Grandmother's shoulders lightly. Her face was pale and waxen in the blue-gold light.

"What did you do?" I cried, unable to look away from her.

"Not a thing," the man answered, sounding much

calmer than me. "Attacking older women isn't my modus operandi. She's simply fainted."

I leaned in close to Grandmother's mouth and nose, not understanding what the man had meant about modus operandi. I wanted to feel Grandmother's breath on my ear. Nothing came. All was still.

"She needs a doctor. Get a doctor!" I cried, finally taking my eyes from her ashen face.

"Please, you have to —!" I sucked in a sharp breath.

The man kneeling beside me was the same man who had been staring at me at the depot, and the one who had been in the back courtyard of Miss Doucette's academy. It was my stranger with the black hat and coat, the defined cheekbones and heart-shaped face.

I shoved myself away from him and landed on my backside.

"You," I whispered. How did this strange man know my grandmother? Why had they been hiding out here talking? Who *was* he?

The stranger stared right back at me. His eyes reminded me of Detective Grogan's: They were acute and intelligent. And his other features . . . up close, his nose, his chin . . . they were so familiar. The memory of something tugged at me from deep inside.

"What now, what's this?" a voice called from the entrance to the music hall. And then, "A woman's collapsed! Is there a doctor here?"

The violin music screeched to a halt and excited murmuring took over. I tore my eyes away from the stranger and looked behind me.

"Yes! She needs help, hurry!" I shouted. People started down the hallway toward us, their dress shoes scuffling over the stone in a furor.

I got up to let a man who claimed to be a doctor have access to Grandmother. The stranger had already retreated down the hallway in the opposite direction, hurrying for the steps that led to the museum's exit.

I was pushed farther outward, away from Grandmother's inert form, as another doctor appeared through the crowd of people.

"Dr. Philbrick!" I exclaimed. He'd been at the concert? He didn't pay me a second's notice but got right on the floor and opened up his doctor's case, which I now assumed he carried with him everywhere.

"Move back!" he shouted. "All of you, move! She needs room to take a decent breath of air."

He waved a small vial beneath Grandmother's nostrils and rolled her to her side to begin unbuttoning the back of her tight-fitting dress, and then the laces on her corset.

"These blasted contraptions. I told her to quit wearing them," Dr. Philbrick grumbled.

Women gasped and shooed their husbands back toward the music hall. The chiming of a bell sounded from that direction, and more people started to return to their abandoned seats.

I was torn. I wanted to stay and see that Grandmother was well again, but I also wanted to chase after the strange man. Why did he keep turning up? What had he meant when he said he had a right to be here? And Grandmother . . . she hadn't wanted him here. She'd seemed to know him.

Grandmother took a ragged breath of air.

"There now, Mrs. Snow, there now," Dr. Philbrick said in a surprisingly soothing way.

He calmed her with more words and encouraged her to lie still another moment. I knelt beside Grandmother so she could see me. Her ice blue eyes were bright and watery.

"Oh, dear," she said softly. "Did I faint again?"

I nodded, trying to keep the tremor from my hand when I sought hers out. I squeezed her small fingers, and suddenly realized what could have happened. That she might not have revived.

Dr. Philbrick packed up his bag and helped Grandmother to her feet.

"Jeremiah, did you unlace me?" she asked indignantly. I tried to lace her back up, but I didn't have the muscle. Bertie must have needed tools to help her every morning.

"Mrs. Snow, you have to be able to breathe!" he replied. "You can't do that when you've got the equivalent of an anaconda snake wrapped around your ribs."

I buttoned her dress as well as I could, leaving the corset loose. She still looked winded and pale. Dr. Philbrick threw his jacket over her shoulders before walking us downstairs to the front door, and then called for our carriage. Within minutes, Grandmother and I were seated across from each other, leaving Dr. Philbrick behind on the sidewalk outside the museum as the horses shuttled forward.

I leaned across the divide and grasped her hand. "What happened?"

"Just one of my episodes, dear." She concentrated on the darkness outside the window.

"No." I squeezed her hand tighter. "It was more than that. There was a man in the corridor with you. I saw him."

Grandmother closed her eyes. "He was no one. No one for you to concern yourself with."

I wondered if I should say something, and decided I had to. "I've seen him before."

The wheels hit something and the whole chassis jerked, compounding Grandmother's surprise.

"That's impossible," she hissed. "That man is a criminal. He's a scoundrel of the worst sort, Suzanna, and I don't know how you could have possibly seen him before."

Grandmother snapped open her fan and began beating the silk ruffles again. Just like she had earlier when I'd brought up the Red Herring Heists. There was something that vexed her about both the old case and the older man who'd been following me around Boston. But I didn't dare question her further, fearing she might faint yet again.

"Of course you're right, Grandmother. Never mind." I watched the color return to her pale cheeks. "He must look like someone I know, that's all. Please, don't worry."

I couldn't bear to see her have another episode, and then not have Dr. Philbrick right at hand.

Grandmother smiled, but it was a sleepy, exhausted smile. "Oh, Zanna, how could I not worry? You're my granddaughter. And your father and mother, they've asked me to take care of you. Protect you. I hope you can understand . . ." She didn't finish her sentence. She leaned her head back against the cushioned panel and closed her fan.

Grandmother needed rest. No stress, Dr. Philbrick had told me. We rode on in silence. She wanted me to understand something, and I did: She was keeping a secret from me. I hoped she could understand something as well: I was going to stop at nothing to find out what the secret was.

Chapter Seven

• • •

Detective Rule: Never overlook the smallest details. They will often lead to the biggest clues.

• • •

MISS DOUCETTE STOOD AT THE FRONT OF THE classroom with pointer in hand. One framed portrait was to her right. A second, nearly identical one was to her left. Both were propped on tall easels so the majority of the class could see. I, however, was seated behind the abnormally tall Lucille, so my view was of her carrot-colored braid.

I didn't mind all that much. Miss Doucette wouldn't be able to see my eyelids drooping come midday. I hadn't slept a wink all night. I'd been nervous Grandmother would suffer from another one of her breathing attacks, and I was also too riled up by meeting the curious stranger face-to-face.

"As you can see, girls, both of these paintings are essentially the same. The only difference is the choice of frames." Miss Doucette whacked her pointer against the plaster molding of the frame I could see.

"This frame, with its ornate carvings and gilded rosettes, is completely unsuitable for the portrait's subject matter," she said.

From what I could see, the subject matter was a light-hued coastal marsh scene. It reminded me of the marshes near Loch Harbor. A tug of homesickness pulled my stomach low, but I quickly chased it away.

"This frame, with its fillet edge and thin brocade of plaster, coated with silver leaf, properly brings out the simplicity of the marshes," Miss Doucette explained. Honestly, I could not tell the difference, but if Miss Doucette said it, it was best to just agree.

Up one row and two seats diagonally from me, Adele sat with crisp posture and her glossy black hair pulled back with ribbons. She was taking notes, and I supposed I should be as well. I did need to learn more about art and framing if I was going to be working on this theory of Adele's. It seemed as if Miss Doucette's lesson for the day was insensitive, what with expensive artworks burning to cinders in the warehouse fires. But other than the Hornes, my uncle, Detective Grogan, and the insurance companies having to process a claim of loss, no one knew about the destroyed art.

"*I* always employ the framer on Kingston Boulevard. He is the finest in Boston," Miss Doucette said before addressing Adele. "I'm sure Mr. Horne has hired Signor Periggi in the past, yes?"

Adele laid her pencil down. "Yes, but my father wasn't pleased with Signor Periggi's work on the Rossetti he purchased last fall. We employ Mr. Dashner."

Miss Doucette looked as though she'd just been slapped. Two dots of crimson bloomed on her cheekbones.

"Oh, well, of course, of course," she stammered. "Yes, Mr. Dashner is also quite accomplished. Let's move on now, girls, and discuss the use of matting."

I couldn't think of anything less exciting than matting. Besides, the mention of framers in Boston had given me an idea. I waited patiently through demonstrations on proper wall mountings until at long last we were all dismissed for the afternoon.

"Adele," I hissed from around the corner of the academy's front, ivy-clad brick wall. She stepped through the open wrought-iron gates and came toward me.

"Are there any remnants?" I asked, and received a quizzical expression in return. "Of the frames? Was there anything left of the art after the fires were put out?"

Adele frowned. "Bits and pieces. Nothing could be salvaged. Why?"

"Did your father or the police keep the pieces?"

"There was no reason to keep them. They were just splinters of wood and ash."

Ash. I recalled the thin coating of ash on Mr. Horne's shoes at the dinner party. If he had gone to one of his ruined warehouses that evening before the party, he might have scuffed his shoes through some ash. But what business could he possibly have at a burned-down warehouse?

Adele held her schoolbooks, tied with a leather strap, closer to her chest. "Have you thought of something?"

"If someone planted fakes in the warehouses before the fires were set, then they must have needed to know the exact dimensions and styles of the frames. Whoever it is wouldn't want to have left behind any remnants of a frame that didn't match what your father had inside the safe box, right?"

If it was theft and not just arson, the thefts would have needed to be premeditated. I liked that word — *premeditated*.

"So whoever it is must have knowledge of the frames. He knew which pieces of art were inside the safe boxes," Adele said, catching on.

A battering wind fanned my excitement. "And he needed to have replica frames made to match the real ones." Then another theory struck. "Or perhaps he made them himself."

Adele twisted up her nose. "Do you think it could be Mr. Dashner, my father's framer?"

It made sense. He knew the frames, had worked with the originals closely. He'd no doubt taken detailed notes on the construction of each frame. Perhaps he'd even advised Mr. Horne on the proper way to store his collection. Mr. Dashner might have even transported them to the warehouses himself.

"I think we should put him down as a possible suspect." I took my notebook from my cloak pocket. "And I think we should visit him soon. Maybe even today. Where is his shop?"

Adele made a strangled gasping sound. "What are we going to do, just waltz in and ask Mr. Dashner if he's a criminal? We need to come up with a better plan than that."

Plans took time. As if *she* could devise the perfect one within a matter of minutes.

"You could pretend you need to have something framed," I suggested. Adele propped a hand on her hip.

"And then what?"

It was a good question, and it stumped me. Maybe there wasn't anything we could do about Dashner yet. First, we had to have something more than just his knowledge of the frames. We needed to know what his motive would be. *Motive* . . . it was another one of my favorite words.

"I think we should check out the illegal underground market," Adele said. It took me by surprise — I'd been thinking about that as well.

Adele looked down the curb to where her brougham and driver waited. She spoke more softly. "Mr. Dashner knows the value of art, doesn't he? He could sell the stolen paintings illegally and make a fortune."

She was right on the mark there. I started to feel a certain kind of kinship with Adele and the way her mind and mine clicked. It was a wary kinship, though. She was so serious and apprehensive, and she watched me as if she expected me to say or do something offensive. Perhaps she thought I was like my uncle? She certainly didn't like him.

I supposed the way my last friendship had ended had made me apprehensive as well. Lucy Kent had been a chambermaid at the Rosemount, and my best friend — until she lied to me and helped in the kidnapping of Maddie Cook.

"But I don't know anything about the underground market," Adele said, her excitement fading. I nodded and admitted I didn't, either.

I wanted there to be an actual, physical underground marketplace, where vendors set up their carts of stolen and illegal goods and shouted out prices. As absurd as the idea was, it would make finding out more information so much easier.

"Will might know," I said, thinking out loud. "But I don't know when I'll see him again. Do you know where Bellmont's Academy is?"

"You can catch up with him tomorrow evening," Adele said. "Papa's having a dinner and I asked if I could invite you and Will. He should be there, along with the detectives and their wives and a few other people," Adele explained, distractedly shuffling her books underneath her arm. "Your grandmother probably received the invitation earlier today."

"Oh," I said. Adele certainly seemed on top of things. "Great."

Adele nodded and then took off down the street without any kind of parting sentiments. Did she want Will and me at her father's dinner in order to discuss the case, or did she want us there as her friends?

I started for Knight Street, finally realizing what it was about Adele that unsettled me. I could pick apart most people, determine their main characteristics, read their body language and their expressions. I couldn't do those things with Adele. And that was what kept me from trusting her completely.

• • •

Adele's house on June Street was exactly what I imagined it would be. Three stories of intricate, patterned brickwork, arched windows, and even a turret and wicked-looking weather vane. Unlike the tightly fitted brownstones lined up along Knight Street, the homes along June each had at least an acre of yard, most of which were fenced in and neatly landscaped with oaks, fountains, and faded summer greenery.

However, the Hornes' lawn was the only one that had statuary. Grandmother's carriage passed through the opened gates, rattled up the short drive, and was greeted by a headless Hercules standing sentry in front of one bay window. A goddess with both arms lost below the elbow had been placed near the bordering hedges, and a cluster of winged and fat-cheeked cherubs with bows and arrows were perched on a center platform in a fountain. Two ancient-looking Egyptian cats with permanent hissing expressions were set on the sides of the front door.

"Not very welcoming," I mentioned. Grandmother lifted her eyebrow at the cats in silent agreement.

The butler led us inside. He was nearly as ancient

as the Egyptian cats. The foyer and stairwell glittered with crystal chandeliers and sconces, gilded frames for portraits and still-life paintings, silk paneled walls and bronze urns potted with lush green shrubbery. I paid close attention to the art as we shed our cloaks and gloves and followed the butler into a room with walls of rich, polished mahogany and green and silver striped wallpaper. A massive crystal chandelier cast a golden glow over everyone and everything inside.

I spotted Adele first, her shiny black hair and snowy complexion turning toward me the moment I stepped in.

"Mother," a deep, rumbling voice called from across the room.

Uncle Bruce stood before the roaring hearth fire in a black suit and tie, his dark, thick head of hair glossed to perfection. He didn't bother with a greeting for me.

"Mrs. Snow!" Xavier Horne said from Uncle Bruce's side. He was wearing a tweed suit, which was less formal than what he'd worn to Grandmother's dinner. As he walked toward us, my eyes instinctively lowered to his shoes. Unlike the ones he'd worn on Saturday evening, these shoes were at a high polish.

Mr. Horne kissed Grandmother's hand. "Jeremiah asked me to see how you were faring. He mentioned you'd had a spell at the museum the other evening."

Jeremiah?

"Do you mean Dr. Philbrick?" I asked, surprised.

"That's right," Mr. Horne answered, reaching for my hand and tickling my skin again with his mustache as he kissed it. "He's a good friend of mine. Jeremiah's collection is just getting under way and we met yesterday at an auction. Tell me, Octavia, are you better since the museum concert?"

Mr. Horne turned back to my grandmother, who seemed embarrassed by all the attention her spell had produced.

Adele came to her father's side. She gave me a tight smile and looked impatient to begin talking about the case with me. Will was perched on a settee by the hearth with a dark-haired, elegantly dressed woman whose diamond earrings and necklace looked like they'd come from straight off the chandelier. The woman was speaking to Will, but he kept flicking his eyes my way, parting his lips to say something, and getting cut off by the woman before he could. I couldn't wait to talk to him about Mr. Dashner and the frames and the underground market. He'd know something, I was sure of it.

"We have to free him from her," Adele said softly. Grandmother and Mr. Horne had stepped away into their own conversation.

"Who is she?" I whispered back.

Adele snorted. "You don't know?"

I shook my head, wondering why Adele should be so amused.

"She's Katherine Snow. Your *aunt*." She practically mouthed the words so no one could overhear.

That was Uncle Bruce's wife! My own aunt. I felt ridiculous for not knowing, but of course I'd never so much as seen a photograph of her.

"We've never met," I explained.

"Clearly," Adele replied. "She adores Will, as you can tell. She'll jabber on at him all evening if we don't tear him away somehow."

I thought to introduce myself. But shouldn't Uncle Bruce or Grandmother do that? I felt invisible and forgotten with all of the adults gathered in a circle by the hearth.

"I hear you have a rare Degas sculpture, Xavier," my grandmother said from within the circle. "Might you treat us with a look?"

Adele gave a small gasp and turned to listen to her father's reply.

"I'm afraid I'm keeping the Degas sculpture under lock and key, Octavia, and its whereabouts secret. I hope you aren't offended."

Grandmother daintily pressed one of her hands to her collar. "Not in the least. But why all the mystery?"

Uncle Bruce's deep tenor followed. "It sounds as if you fear for the thing's security."

I slid my eyes over to Adele and watched her bite her lower lip.

"Of course I fear for its security. That *thing* is my collection's crown jewel, Detective. I would never keep my entire collection under one roof, and I most certainly don't think it's wise for a collector to advertise the location of a piece as rare as my Degas." Mr. Horne chuckled, as if any simpleton would know to do the same.

My uncle understood his silent meaning entirely too well. He pinched his lips tightly. "Do you mean to say you're worried about the security of the remainder of your art collection? I can assure you, the location is safe. The burglary at the Philbrick place was an odd sort of coincidence."

The Philbrick place? I tugged on Adele's arm, jarring her from her intense eavesdropping. "The paintings were stolen from Dr. Philbrick's home?"

Looking just as surprised, she answered, "I didn't know where they were being stored." Adele lowered her voice, her surprise changing to frustration. "My father isn't telling me anything. I don't understand why."

Adele broke eye contact with me and looked away.

"Have you heard what else was taken in the burglary?" I asked.

But just then, Detective Grogan entered the receiving room, announced by the Hornes' butler. The woman on Detective Grogan's arm stole my attention, and Adele's as well. For good reason, too: She was stunning.

"Neil! Hannah!" Mr. Horne exclaimed in greeting.

Hannah, who must have been Detective Grogan's wife, was young, pretty, and wore her strawberry blond hair twisted in a loose chignon. She wore a chic, body-hugging black dress that sported a V-shaped neck instead of a high collar.

Grandmother pinched her lips with disapproval over so much exposed skin and shapeliness. I thought she looked lovely, though. And sophisticated. The way Adele smiled — genuinely, at that — and moved forward to welcome Hannah warmly, told me she was impressed by Detective Grogan's wife as well.

Hannah's arrival was what ended up tearing my aunt Katherine from Will's side on the settee. The two women embraced and complimented each other's dresses, and Will broke for our sides.

"Thank goodness," he whispered. "I thought I'd have to listen to her talk about her trip to Venice for the entire evening. So what's happening, Zanna? Adele told me when I first got here you had a lead."

I checked to be sure the adults were properly ignoring us. Satisfied, I ushered Will and Adele closer to a wall of built-in bookshelves, the shelves shuttered with glass doors. I watched the group of adults in the glass's reflection as I explained to Will about Mr. Dashner and the theory that he might have sold the art illegally.

"I don't know a whole lot about the underground market," Will said quietly. "But Detective Grogan might. That's been his thing the last few years, though not for stolen art. More like machinery and weapons and nicked warehouse goods."

I glanced into the bookcase's glass and saw Neil Grogan adjust the eyeglasses on the bridge of his nose. He nodded at something Uncle Bruce was saying.

"You could ask him about the burglary at Dr. Philbrick's house," Adele suggested. "I'm sure he'd know what else was stolen."

I bet he'd also know about another case, too. One I was much more interested in at the moment.

"The Red Herring Heists," I said, perhaps a bit too loudly. There was a momentary pause in the flow of adult conversation. But it picked up again quickly.

"The case Grogan was talking about at your grandmother's," Will said. "You could pretend to be interested in that old case and then dig some information on the underground market out of him, too. Brilliant, Zanna."

I would have accepted Will's praise had I not noticed a fourth addition to our grouping by the bookshelves. I hadn't caught his approach in the glass's reflection, but now he stood directly behind us.

Detective Grogan cleared his throat. "Now, what's all this about the underground market?"

Chapter Eight

• • •

Detective Rule: Always keep an eye on your peripherals.

• • •

I TURNED TOWARD DETECTIVE GROGAN RELUCtantly, knowing my cheeks and ears would be aflame. Surprisingly enough, Grogan's own face looked like a newly ripening tomato. A trickle of sweat rolled down his temple and he loosened the tie around his neck. Come to think of it, the receiving room *was* warm.

"Oh, we were just talking about that case," I answered. "The one you mentioned the other evening . . . what was it, the Red Robin Heists?"

Perhaps it had been a bit much — a cool look from Adele confirmed it. But Detective Grogan didn't seem fazed.

"The Red *Herring* Heists," he corrected. "What was it about the case that interested you?"

Unprepared for that one, I opened my mouth to reply. Nothing exited. Blast.

"Was it ever solved?" Adele piped up.

Grogan took a handkerchief from his suit pocket and dabbed his beading forehead.

"No. The heists are a cold case," he answered.

"That means it's unsolved," Adele said. I glanced at her. She certainly knew her detective terminology.

Grogan put down his handkerchief and grinned. "That's correct, Miss Horne. One day the art heists simply stopped, and the trail went cold. The police had a prime suspect at one point, but he eluded capture. The investigation went on for a short while after that, though nothing ever came of it. And no other museums or homes were ever burgled to provide more clues. Simple as that, really."

By Grogan's smooth, nearly wrinkle-free face I estimated him at thirty years of age or younger.

"You weren't on the force when the heists took place," I said. He smiled, almost bashfully.

"No, I'm afraid I was only just graduating from Bellmont's," he answered with a nod toward Will. "But I heard the stories and read the reports when I joined the force a handful of years later. Your uncle, though —" Grogan swung an arm out to gesture to Uncle Bruce. "Detective Snow was a rising star on the force at the time. He was part of the investigation. You might want to talk to him, rather than me."

Talk to Uncle Bruce about a case? That was a bit unlikely.

"Oh, no, that's not necessary. I was more curious about why someone would steal a well-known painting to begin with. The thief couldn't exactly go and hang it in his study or hallway," I said with a false giggle. Adele and Will joined me. We sounded pathetic. But once again, Grogan didn't pick up on it. He grimaced and loosened his tie even further.

"No, art isn't stolen for its beauty, but for its value. The thief most likely sold the items unlawfully in the underground market."

"What happens then?" Adele asked.

"The thief seeks a buyer. Usually, it's all done anonymously. The buyer doesn't know the seller and vice versa."

"Oh," I said, still confused. "But how do they find each other? Is there some kind of underground market directory?"

I instantly wanted to take the inane question back. Of course there wasn't a directory! Grogan chuckled.

"Something like that," he said, laughing again. He looked as if he was about to say something more enlightening when his wife, Hannah, took him by the arm. She eyed his sweaty pallor.

"You're still not feeling well, Neil?"

He shrugged off her concern with a nonchalant grin. "This is Hannah, my wife," Grogan said to me. "Hannah, this is Bruce's niece, Suzanna. She's visiting from Canada."

Hannah reached out both of her hands and closed them around mine. She gave them a squeeze.

"Of course! Katherine has told me all about you," she said breathlessly.

"She has?" I asked, stunned. I hadn't even met my aunt yet.

Hannah laughed. "You simply must sit beside me at dinner tonight. I don't care if we have to reshuffle the entire seating arrangement. Even if Neil and Bruce end up beside each other and talk shop all night, it will be worth it. I have to hear everything about the Cook case."

Oh. The Cook case. Of course. But I didn't want to think about that old case. The stranger who'd tipped off Adele to the art theft theory had mentioned the *red herrings had returned*. And the Red Herring Heists had involved stolen art. There was a connection there. Why hadn't my uncle — or Detective Grogan for that matter — picked up on that?

Detective Grogan bowed out of the group, heading for a window. He opened the sash a few inches and breathed in a gust of cold autumn air just as Aunt Katherine, her ears and neck and fingers shimmering with gaudy baubles, joined us.

"Don't be silly, Hannah darling. The boys can't sit next to each other. They'll bore the rest of us to death with their police talk."

Will began to introduce me to her. "Aunt Katherine, this is —"

"Suzanna. It's wonderful to meet you at last. Bruce has told me so much about you."

My heart seized. He had? Oh no. What had he said? The way Aunt Katherine's inflexible gaze took me in from head to toe, I gathered it couldn't have been anything very flattering. I managed to stammer how nice it was to meet her as well, before the dinner bell, mercifully, cut me off.

She and Hannah turned to join their husbands, leaving Will, Adele, and me alone. Adele didn't waste a moment.

"I need to protect the rest of my papa's artworks," she whispered. We hung back, slowly following the adults. Detective Grogan was the first to disappear through the rolled-open pocket doors, Hannah at his side. I waited until Mr. Horne followed Grandmother and Uncle Bruce out of the room and into the foyer, leaving the three of us by ourselves.

"Uncle Bruce said the rest of your father's art was safe and sound in its new location," I replied. "I'm guessing neither of you knows where it was taken?"

Adele shook her head. Will did the same. I was sure there was plenty of valuable art right here in the house on June Street. Mr. Horne didn't seem worried about it, though, at least not like he had about that Degas sculpture.

"The Degas," I whispered aloud.

"The one Adele's father is keeping under lock and key," Will added. I flashed him a smile. He was supposed to have been chatting with Aunt Katherine, not eavesdropping like Adele and I.

We both looked to Adele. She took an extra-long moment to begin.

"It was my mother's most cherished piece. My father's, too. It's a preliminary statue Edgar Degas sculpted to prepare for his *Little Dancer* statue. You must have seen his *Little Dancer* before, haven't you, Zanna?"

I wished I had, but exposure to fine art was a rarity back home.

"Why is it so special?" I asked instead.

"Because hardly anyone in the world knows it even exists," Adele answered. "My father once said it would be worth an unbelievable fortune, but that's not why he loves it. It's the secret of it he loves so much, I think.

He never displays it and moves it from safe to safe regularly. *I've* only laid eyes on it once or twice myself."

If an art thief knew about the existence of this rare Degas, I imagined it could be a prime target. I listed who would know about the Degas: my uncle and his department, Adele, the Horne house servants perhaps. Adele confirmed the list, also saying a close handful of collectors her father associated with had probably seen it. Then a speculation struck me.

"Does Mr. Dashner know about the Degas?" I asked.

"Yes," she answered. "Papa has the Degas cleaned every year and Mr. Dashner does it."

A proper theory was taking shape and my head spun with it. We then heard the sound of shoes tapping along the polished hallway floor.

"What about the other paintings? The ones that were removed from the warehouses," I went on. "Would Mr. Dashner have known they'd been moved?"

The footsteps down the hallway sounded closer. Someone was coming to fetch us.

"Yes," she answered again. I saw the light of striking gold in her wide eyes. "Since Papa was already moving the pieces, he thought it would be a good time to have the frame for a Cézanne regilded. He had Mr. Dashner meet him at Noone's Wharf to pick it up!"

At that moment, Adele's dour, prune-faced butler found us huddled in the receiving room.

"Dinner, Miss Adele. May I escort you and your friends to your seats?"

It was an order masked by politeness — he was the butler, but he ran the house. My mind galloped in circles as we were led to the dining room. Mr. Dashner knew about the existence of the Degas, and that the paintings had been taken from the safe boxes. He probably knew where they were being held as well. But did he know where Mr. Horne had stashed the Degas?

We entered the dining room just as Detective Grogan was exiting.

"I'll fetch your coat, Detective," the butler said with a slight bow.

Grogan was still blotchy and sweating profusely.

"You're leaving?" I asked. He didn't need to answer, really. He looked ready to vomit all over the Persian carpet.

Grogan raised his thin, light-colored eyebrows and tried to smile at Adele. "I apologize, Miss Horne." He then turned to me. "Let me know if you're still curious about the Red Herring Heists, Suzanna. I'll see if I can pull the files for you if they're public."

I said thank you and then Detective Grogan was gone. Nearly all the others had taken their seats at the table, including Hannah. A suited footman pulled out the chair beside hers and bowed toward me. She'd managed to switch the seating arrangement after all. I slipped into the chair, dreading having to talk yet again about the Maddie Cook case.

"The Red Herring Heists?" Hannah asked, having overheard her husband. "Why, I don't think I've heard of that case before."

Uncle Bruce was settling down into his seat across from me. He snatched the cloth napkin away from the footman who was trying to place it in his lap.

"Why are you asking about that case?" he barked. I was quickly learning that the ability to hide his feelings was not one of Uncle Bruce's strengths.

"It just caught my interest," I replied. He held my gaze another moment but didn't make a reply. He cut his eyes away from me and sent a fast glance down the table. They landed on Grandmother. I followed the look and saw she also had a drawn expression. When she saw me watching her, she painted on a smile.

Hannah began asking questions about the Cook case, and I answered dutifully. Every now and then I heard an irritated sigh or throat clearing from across the table. Uncle Bruce tried to redirect the conversation, asking Mr. Horne about business, imploring his wife to regale us with stories of Venice, and even going so far as to ask Will how Bellmont's was going for him this year. As if Uncle Bruce actually *cared*.

I didn't pay any attention to it really, because it wasn't the Cook case I wanted to be talking, or even thinking, about. It was the Red Herring Heists that were now firmly nagging at me. Uncle Bruce and Grandmother didn't like my interest in them. And that, naturally, only made me want to know more.

• • •

Bertie had a pot of tea ready for us when we arrived home. We unwrapped ourselves in the foyer and went into the parlor, where a fire licked the hearth logs and a plush chair beckoned me. Grandmother sat back in her chair and lifted her small feet onto a low, ruffled footstool.

"Miss Zanna, you've a telegram," Bertie said, placing the rectangular envelope on the sofa's end table.

"They certainly miss you," Grandmother said, her lids closing in exhaustion.

My parents did seem to be overdoing the correspondence a little, and I was running out of things to say in my responses that didn't involve the case. Thank goodness telegrams required short sentences. But I had to give my parents some leeway. It was my first time away from home, and my father hadn't even wanted me to go in the first place. I put the telegram in my skirt pocket and accepted a cup of tea from Bertie.

"Grandmother," I began. "Why do you think my father dislikes Boston so much?"

I couldn't imagine it had anything to do with her. Grandmother wasn't overbearing or mean or someone to avoid at all costs.

"Dislike?" she echoed. Her eyes fluttered open. "I don't know what you mean. Why would Benjamin dislike his hometown?"

I sipped the peppermint tea. Grandmother also wasn't a very good liar.

"He never visits," I said.

"He's a very busy man." Her immediate excuse had the worn, overused quality of something she'd said time and again. Much like my answers to questions about the Maddie Cook case.

Grandmother closed her eyes again, but her relaxed posture in the chair had turned slightly rigid. I sensed she was waiting to see if I'd give up. She really should have known better.

"My father didn't want me to visit. He said it was too dangerous. Why would he think that?"

She flapped away my question with a tired sweep of her hand. "I'm sure I have no idea. My house is far from dangerous and I am completely capable of seeing to your protection."

I set my teacup on its saucer and balanced it on my lap. "Protection from what?"

Grandmother's lids sprang open. Her startled, caught-red-handed expression threw me back to that evening around the Horne table.

"Both you and Uncle Bruce reacted so strangely when I brought up the Red Herring Heists tonight. Won't you tell me what it is about that case that frightens the two of you?"

I hadn't known those were the words I was going to choose. The question of what frightened them about the cold case made Grandmother sit forward and look me in the eye.

"Frightens us? That's absurd, Zanna. We aren't frightened by some dusty old case that no one has thought of for over a dozen years."

I didn't believe her. Uncle Bruce had just about burned me with his scathing stare, and Grandmother had paled drastically. The same way she had at her own dinner party last weekend, when Mr. Horne had asked me about my middle name. I sat straighter, nearly spilling my tea onto my lap.

"You both reacted strangely then, too," I said softly to myself. Grandmother frowned.

"When?"

I set my cup on a low table and stood up.

"At your dinner party, when Mr. Horne wanted to know my middle name. You interrupted to say you'd heard the dinner bell chiming —" I took a breath, figuring something out. "But you hadn't really heard it, had you? You made it up. The servants were all surprised to find us in the dining room. They hadn't rung the bell, and you knew it." I pointed my finger at her even though I knew I shouldn't. "You lied. You jumped in and lied to keep me from saying my middle name."

Grandmother opened her mouth to reply, but instead shut it and dipped her head. It was as good as an admission of guilt.

"You don't want me to ask about the Red Herring Heists, and you don't want anyone to know Leighton is my middle name. Why?"

I decided to give her a few moments, even a full minute, to gather her response. I was on the right track, but I didn't want to push her. She wasn't fanning herself or looking breathless, but I didn't want to take the chance of having her collapse and stop breathing. I waited. The only noise was that of the hearth fire and of a fast-moving carriage coming up Knight Street.

She looked up and met my patient stare. "Suzanna, I understand that you're full of questions. I know you aspire to be a detective, too, like Bruce. You're well on your way already." A fleeting grin lifted her serious expression. "If you weren't so astute, you never would have noticed anything amiss. I won't treat you like a simple child, but I also can't tell you everything. The truth involves many —"

A few hoarse shouts came from outside the parlor windows. The slam of a carriage door interrupted the confession I'd nearly won from Grandmother. A fist thumped heavily on the brownstone's front door. Bertie raced to the foyer, her starched cotton skirts swishing loudly at the incessant pounding.

"Mr. Snow!" Bertie exclaimed, and within a second Uncle Bruce was inside the parlor. He looked from Grandmother to me, his eyes blazing, his hair disheveled. The white shirt he'd worn that night under his suit jacket was streaked with sweat and soot.

"My goodness, Bruce, what on earth has happened to you?" Grandmother went to him and he grasped her arms tightly.

"You're all right?" He swiveled toward Grandmother's stunned servant. "Bertie, have you or Margaret Mary seen anyone strange lurking about tonight? Anyone at all?"

Bertie shook her head, her white-gloved hands clasped together at her lace collar.

"Bruce, what's the matter? What's wrong?" Grandmother asked again.

He let go of his mother's arms and went to the hearth, pacing in front of the flames. Grandmother and I watched, waiting for an answer. He braced himself against the mantel and hung his head low, his back turned to us.

"Bertie, some more tea," Grandmother said quietly, but Uncle Bruce whipped around.

"No tea, Mother, not now. My God," he said, his voice hoarse, as if he'd been shouting. "It's Neil. His home . . . it's gone. Burned. Burned to the foundation and —"

He shook his head, ran his hand through his thick black hair. A new emotion played across his face, one I had not yet seen: anguish.

"And we fear Neil has burned with it."

My knees gave out. I collapsed into the seat of my chair. Grandmother gasped and whimpered.

"No! Oh no, tell me it's not true!" she cried.

Detective Grogan was . . . was dead? I couldn't believe it. I didn't *want* to believe it. Tears smarted in my eyes and blurred the parlor, which was already dim in the firelight.

"That's not all, either," Uncle Bruce continued. "My home is gone as well."

Grandmother all-out screamed this time. She fell onto the sofa, thankfully caught and guided by Uncle Bruce.

"It's all right, Mother, no one was injured there. I'd dismissed the servants earlier in the evening since we were attending the dinner at Xavier's."

I sat immobile, my limbs numb. But my mind raced with questions.

"Both of your homes were set on fire during the dinner party?" I asked.

Uncle Bruce nodded. "It looks that way. Perhaps retaliation from the Irish mob for all of the investigating we've been doing on the Horne fires. We'd just brought in one of their higher-ups for questioning." Uncle Bruce closed his eyes, no doubt thinking of his partner.

"So you think they somehow knew you'd be gone from your homes tonight?" I asked.

"Except Neil had felt ill. . . . He'd gone home early . . ." Uncle Bruce couldn't finish his sentence. He dipped his head and worked the muscles in his jaw.

Grandmother seemed to lift from her shock. "Great heavens, Neil's wife. Poor Hannah, where is she? Is she all right?"

Uncle Bruce, now sitting beside his mother, nodded heavily. "She and Katherine are at Will's mother's home. The police and fire crew didn't want her near the scene. . . . She was in hysterics, trying to get inside while the house was crumbling."

I didn't want to consider it possible that Neil Grogan was dead. Perhaps he'd gone to call on a doctor before going home, or a pharmacy. Perhaps he'd not been at home like everyone feared.

"Have they found the — the body yet?" I asked, lowering my voice when I said "body." It seemed so disrespectful to refer to a man I'd just spoken to earlier in the evening as a "body."

Uncle Bruce shook his head and stood.

"No, but I must get back to the scene. When they do, I should be there. And then I need to pay a visit to Xavier." He ran a hand through his messed hair. "On top of everything else lost tonight are the paintings we'd moved from his warehouses. We thought Neil's house would be safer. We thought . . ." But he couldn't finish. He made a face, scrunching up his eyes and nose to block tears.

That was where they'd taken the paintings? And now Detective Grogan's home had been burned. It couldn't be a coincidence.

"I just needed to be sure you were all right, Mother," Uncle Bruce said once he'd recovered. "With two homes burning, I worried those criminals might have targeted other people connected to Neil or me."

Grandmother blotted her eyes and tear-streaked cheeks with her lace handkerchief.

"Of course, Bruce, of course. Oh, I just can't believe —" She gasped sharply. I jumped up.

"Grandmother, are you feeling all right? Do you need me to call for Dr. Philbrick?"

She shook her head. "No, no. I'm fine, just devastated. Devastated," she repeated. "Bruce dear, I won't keep you. Thank you for coming."

Uncle Bruce hesitated, eyeing his mother warily. He then stooped to kiss her cheek.

"Please rest, Mother, and don't work yourself into a panic. I've got two officers on watch out front just in case. I'll be back in the morning if I can."

He left the sofa, and as he passed me, said beneath his breath, "Make sure she rests, Suzanna. I'm depending on you."

He flinched, as if he hadn't meant to say the last part. But then, knowing he couldn't take the words back, darted out of the parlor.

Grandmother sat on the sofa quietly sniffling into her handkerchief. Bertie came in with more tea. Smartly, she'd brought one of Dr. Philbrick's prescribed tonics as well.

Grandmother sipped while I sat trying to wrap my mind around every aspect of the tragic news Uncle

Bruce had just delivered. Detective Grogan was feared to be dead. His and Uncle Bruce's homes lay in burned shambles, and there was one more loss to deal with on top of it all.

The paintings removed from Mr. Horne's warehouses for safekeeping had ended up being destroyed anyway. Any normal person might have chalked it up to irony, bad luck, or fate. But I wasn't a normal person. I was a detective-at-large. And I was angry.

"I'm going to solve this, Detective Grogan," I whispered into my tea. "I promise."

Chapter Nine

• • •

Sat., Sept. 26, 10 a.m., Varden St., Lawton Square:

Dashner's shop closed up tight, same as yester day and the day before. Possibilities: (1) On holiday, (2) In hospital, (3) On the lam with priceless works of art.

Partial to possibility #3.

• • •

I'D BEEN STAKING OUT MR DASHNER'S SHOP front for three days. Well, more like sneaking past his shop on my way home from school. His shop on Varden Street was just a block out of my way, and after what had happened Tuesday night, I'd needed to get cracking on this investigation.

Detective Grogan's death and the twin fires had been splashed all over the front page of every Boston newspaper for days. His body — or what remained of it — had been discovered at daybreak the morning after the fire. More members of the underground mob had been arrested, questioned, and ultimately released.

None of the charges were sticking to anyone, and Uncle Bruce was livid. He and Aunt Katherine were staying at the Copley Square Hotel, one of the nicest hotels in Boston. Still, each time he came to Grandmother's brownstone, he looked worse and worse. To my great astonishment, I'd started to feel sorry for him.

He'd lost his partner and his home, and his investigation was a disaster. It couldn't get any more dreadful than that. I closed my notebook and put it back in my pocket. Actually, I supposed it could. Neil Grogan's funeral was in just two hours. I had never been to a funeral before, but Grandmother said we must attend to show our support and sorrow. Of course, I agreed, but still . . . I was a bit nervous. Just like when Adele told me about her mother being dead, what could I possibly say to Hannah to make her feel better? *I'm sorry* wasn't enough.

To work out my nerves, I'd told Grandmother I was going to run to the florist on Kingston Boulevard and purchase some roses for Hannah. Perhaps I could just hand her those and not have to say anything at all. Plus, the florist was just one block shy of Mr. Dashner's shop. Grandmother had said that Bertie could go, but I'd insisted. Grandmother had been too preoccupied with getting ready for the funeral to argue.

I checked my pocket watch to see how much time I'd wasted going to Mr. Dashner's. Not too bad. The rain from last night's storm had lightened to a mist, but the runoff in the street gutters was still fast. I didn't mind the rain. It cleared away most of the horse manure at least. And the dreary weather seemed fitting for a funeral.

I snapped my pocket watch closed, but the rain had made the silver wet and the whole thing slipped from my hand. The watch *tinked* off the pavement. With a gasp, I crouched to retrieve it, hoping the glass face hadn't cracked or the slim hands been damaged. No sooner had I picked up the watch and started to stand than I saw a glimpse of the sidewalk behind me. My eyes landed on Adele Horno, who stood, stock-still, just ten paces away.

"Adele?" I said, rising up from my crouch. She had the distinct look of someone who'd been caught in the act. But what act? Had she been *following* me?

"Oh. Suzanna. H-hello."

I searched the street for her father, or the stylish brougham that dropped her off and picked her up every day at the academy. I didn't see either.

"What are you doing on Varden Street?" I asked, walking back toward her.

Adele repositioned her gray, felted muffin-shaped hat. I'd never seen her wear it nor the plain gray wool jacket that looked to be a size too big for her. If she hadn't wanted me to spot her, and perhaps even wanted to blend in with the crowds on this gray morning, she'd chosen the right ensemble to wear.

"What are *you* doing on Varden Street?" she shot back defensively.

I put my pocket watch away, this time successfully. "You were following me."

Adele's usually icy expression flushed.

"Well, I thought we were going to be solving this case together," she replied, still bristling. "You've been staking out Mr. Dashner's shop for days and not once did you think to —"

Adele stopped and bottled up the rest of her sentence. She didn't need to finish. I hadn't thought to invite her.

"I didn't think . . ." I shrugged. What could I say? Adele was right: I *hadn't* thought to invite her. "Look, I'm sorry. It didn't cross my mind, but it should have. I suppose I'm just used to doing things by myself."

The pinch of Adele's lips loosened. "Well . . . I see Mr. Dashner's shop is still closed. Where are you going now?"

I still had my excuse to Grandmother to hold up. "The florist's. I'm getting flowers for the funeral." Adele began walking with me toward the corner of Kingston Boulevard. "Are you going?"

She was quiet as we rounded the corner. I took a covert glance her way.

"I don't like funerals," she finally said. I imagined it had something to do with her mother's death. I didn't want to ask, though.

"I wouldn't think many people do," I replied as the florist's colorful striped awnings came into view. Another sign then grabbed my attention.

I halted and stared at the rectangular sign hanging from a bar just above the shop's door. The wooden sign had been engraved with one name: PERIGGI. The single display window showed off frames of all sizes and shapes and colors.

"Signor Periggi," I whispered, my lips cocking into a smile.

"*One of the finest framers in Boston*," Adele said in a startlingly pitch-perfect imitation of Miss Doucette. I stared at her, shocked. Not only had she actually just said something funny, but she'd also recalled our teacher's exact wording from earlier that week. Adele muffled a laugh.

"I think I have an idea," I said, and began to cross the rain-washed street. Adele chased after me, careful to avoid buggies and carriages and delivery bicycles.

"Care to share it with me this time?" she asked.

I peered inside Signor Periggi's shopwindow. "There can't be too many custom framers in Boston. Maybe Signor Periggi knows Mr. Dashner. Maybe he even knows where Mr. Dashner has disappeared to."

I opened the front door. A rigged bell chimed above our heads as we walked in. The shop smelled of oil and sanded wood, paint, and a certain musty scent that could only be described as "age."

A small man glanced up from a crowded worktable in the far corner of the one-room shop. "May I help you?"

He wore goggles that magnified both of his eyes, and his long black hair had been messily pulled back with a ribbon. He squinted at me, his enlarged eyes comical until he took off his goggles.

"Hello," I said, trying to sound innocent. "Are you Signor Periggi?"

The man put his goggles down and came out from behind the workbench. He wore a long leather apron streaked with grease and a glittery substance — gilt perhaps.

"Sì, my name is Periggi. Francesco Periggi. May I ask how I can assist such charming young ladies?"

Signor Periggi's English was good, but he still spoke with an Italian accent. I needed to listen carefully.

"We're . . . we're looking to have something framed for our grandmother," I lied, quickly trying to think of more. "For her birthday. A painting. We thought we'd use Dashner's Framery, but it's been closed up for days."

I wanted to lead Signor Periggi to tell us something — anything — about Mr. Dashner. That he wasn't an honest dealer, or that we should stay away from him for some reason or another. Something to fuel my theory. But Periggi didn't oblige me.

"Dashner is away on holiday, I believe. If your grandmother's present can wait until Monday, I suggest trying his shop then. He does very nice work, and —" Periggi waved at the packed back portion of the shop. "As you can see, I am quite occupied at the moment. I've just finished a large *commissione* for a client and now I must return to my others."

"Commissione?" I wasn't proficient in French and definitely not in Italian.

"A commission. A job," he explained. "Many frames built over the last few weeks. All for one *difficile* — ah, picky? — client. But now, Signor Periggi is finished!" He brushed his hands together and waved them away. "You will try Mr. Dashner Monday?"

Adele and I nodded glumly, both of us disappointed not to have uncovered anything gritty. But I did need to get those flowers.

"Thank you, Signor Periggi," Adele said, opening the door. "I'm glad you're finished with your *difficile* client, too."

Her accent was spot on. Periggi bellowed a laugh as we stepped outside. "*Sì!* Eleven frames from scratch in less than two months . . . *pazzo!* Crazy!"

I popped my head in. "Did you say you had an order for eleven frames?"

"No, *sedici* — sixteen. But I ended up only needing to finish eleven."

I stepped back into the shop and sent the bell chiming again. My mind raced to tally up the number of paintings lost in both the warehouse fires and in Grogan's house fire. Three had been "lost" in the first fire, two in the second blaze, then four stolen from Dr. Philbrick's house, and six more supposedly burned just last Tuesday. That came to fifteen. I checked my notebook to be sure. Yes. Fifteen paintings in all, not eleven.

I shoved the notebook back into my cloak pocket, disappointed yet again. I'd been eager to find a clue, but I already knew most suspicions didn't pan out. Signor Periggi observed me quizzically.

"Your client must own a museum," Adele said, and right away I knew it wasn't to fill the awkward moment of silence. Was she trying to question him as well?

The framer shook his head. "Perhaps. I do not know him very well."

I could almost see the cogs and wheels inside Adele's head turning to think of a tricky way to ask who the client was. But the number of frames was too high anyway. The small clock mounted on the wall of Periggi's shop alerted us to the time.

"Thank you, Signor Periggi," I said with a tug on Adele's arm. "Good day."

I closed the door behind us, turned around, and nearly collided with Jeremiah Philbrick.

"Miss Snow?" he said, his bushy eyebrows furrowing downward. "Miss Horne?"

"Dr. Philbrick," we replied in unison. He looked around, apparently searching for Grandmother or Mr. Horne. "My grandmother is at home. Getting ready for the funeral."

"Father, too," Adele added.

He coughed. "Yes, of course. But what were you two doing inside the framer's shop?"

I wasn't about to tell him the truth. "Just checking on prices. A gift for Grandmother, maybe."

He wrinkled up his lips, pressing them hard together in doubt.

"Did you know Detective Grogan?" I asked to distract him.

He sighed and reached for the knob to Periggi's shop, but then drew back his hand as if he'd realized he wasn't going inside that shop anyway. "I did not. I simply looked over the . . . ah . . . remains."

He said the word *remains* with a small, respectful bow of his head.

Adele took both Dr. Philbrick and me by surprise with a question: "But didn't Detective Grogan investigate the burglary at your house?"

Of course! He must have met Detective Grogan before. A hoarse grumble worked its way up Dr. Philbrick's throat.

"That doesn't mean I *knew* the man." Again, he reached for the door to Periggi's shop. Again, he drew it away, flustered. "Now, if you'll excuse me. Good day, ladies."

He tipped his hat and continued on down the sidewalk. Adele stared after him, a triumphant gleam in her otherwise steely eyes.

"Well, something ruffled his feathers. Do you think it was the way we caught him in a lie?"

Dr. Philbrick had definitely seemed disconcerted. But I knew better than to jump to conclusions. He'd had a sound point about his relationship with Detective Grogan. . . . He hadn't truly known him. He'd barely been acquainted with him.

"We don't have any proof he lied," I answered. "But that was a clever catch you made, remembering the burglary."

Adele didn't seem to know whether to thank me for the compliment or to ignore it altogether. We walked a few paces toward the florist's, Adele taking distracted glances behind us.

"Trying to work Signor Periggi for information about Mr. Dashner wasn't so bad an idea, either," she returned.

The exchange of terse compliments left me feeling fidgety. I couldn't help but feel awkward around Adele. She had such a stony, grave manner. But at the same time, I sensed that she wanted to be around me. She'd followed me to Varden Street, after all.

"So the trolley is back there. I should go," she said, quickly reversing her direction. "And you need to get those flowers still."

She took another searching glance behind her, and I figured out what she was up to. "You're going to follow Dr. Philbrick, aren't you?"

Adele's eyes popped wide, but then cleared back over to a calm gray. "Who says you get to be the only detective around here?"

If not for the slight lift of her lips, I might have taken that as an accusation. But Adele all but hopped away and down the sidewalk in the opposite direction in pursuit of Grandmother's physician. So Adele wanted to be a detective, too, did she? I hurried to the florist's shop, trying to think of all the reasons the idea was absurd. I couldn't settle on a single one. The truth was, with her cool composure, quick thinking, and aloof personality, Adele Horne would make a fine sleuth. Whether or not that also made her a fine friend was still undecided. I supposed, in the end, it didn't matter. We had a case to solve.

But first, I had a funeral to attend.

● ● ●

The service was strangely calming. Mourners spoke in hushed tones and shed tears silently, and scores of uniformed officers who had turned out to pay their respects to Detective Grogan wore somber, unshakable expressions. I spent the majority of the service, held inside St. Sebastian's Church of the Holy Christ, worrying what I would say should I come face-to-face with

Hannah Grogan. I'd pricked my restless fingers on the thorns of the roses I'd purchased at least a half-dozen times.

I needn't have worried. She was surrounded by people she'd known far longer than me, and didn't so much as notice I was there. Uncle Bruce sat beside her in the front pew, his broad shoulders mammoth compared to her small, quivering ones. He held her close to his side, whispering supportive words no doubt, while Aunt Katherine sat stone-faced on Uncle Bruce's other side. Will was there, too, sitting with his parents near Aunt Katherine. I didn't have a chance to speak to him until after the service.

We followed far behind the pallbearers who carried Detective Grogan's casket into the cemetery behind the church.

"Have you seen Adele?" I asked, searching the rest of the line of mourners. Mr. Horne was just ahead of us, but Adele's shiny black curls were not beside him.

The calm voice of logic kept insisting she hadn't come because she "didn't like funerals." But the anxious voice of worry kept inventing all sorts of dangerous scenarios in which she'd tangled herself up while following Dr. Philbrick.

"No. Why?" Will asked.

"She went a bit Sherlock on me this morning." Then in hushed tones, I relayed everything that had happened.

"Dr. Philbrick is a friend of Mr. Horne's, isn't he?" Will asked. I nodded. "Maybe Adele's had run-ins with him before. It could have given her an upper hand with her suspicions of him."

That didn't help the anxious voice slowly growing louder and louder in my ear. Will saw my worry.

"We'll try and find her after the burial, okay?"

I nodded, grateful to have Will there to talk me out of a panic. Detectives didn't panic. That had to be one of my top Detective Rules.

The procession came to a stop around the burial site. And that was when I saw him: the strange man who'd been following me.

He was standing behind one of the many tall gray stone pillars that marked the graves. I took a fast scan of the mourners, all clad in black and gray and brown, and it looked as if he was succeeding in going unnoticed. That is, by everyone but me.

I paid extra attention to Grandmother, peering at her through my side vision, worrying she would see him and collapse into a fit. So far, though, she seemed to be oblivious to his presence.

The casket had been placed on the lowering device and the crowd had gathered around closely to hear the priest speak. I wanted to go to the stranger and demand to know who he was, but I also knew I should stay and listen to the final words being said in Detective Grogan's honor. Grandmother flanked me to the right, and Will to the left, and I knew there would be no escaping.

Prayers and words about acceptance and grieving and keeping the fond memories of the dearly departed slipped into one ear and out the other. I could only focus on the stranger hiding in the cemetery, watching. Why was he here?

I'd read in plenty of detective novels that the perpetrators of crimes sometimes enjoyed watching the effects of their misdeeds. Could that be what he was doing? Had he been the one to set the fires? I tossed the idea around as the priest's eulogy wrapped up, and the hush of whispering and sniffling took over once again.

The funeral was over. That was it. No wonder Adele hadn't come. Now the world should just move on, minus one good man? The idea made my heart sink even lower, and it also fanned my anger.

"Zanna, darling, we should hurry home. The funeral reception will be beginning, and I need to be sure Margaret Mary has things under control." Grandmother took my arm and started to guide me back along the grassy footpath to the tall cemetery gates.

"Grandmother, I'm worried about Adele," I said, and sent a fast, hard glance toward Will, urging him to follow along. "I think Will and I should walk over to June Street to see if she doesn't want to come to the reception after all. It isn't very far from here."

Grandmother cupped my cheek in her palm, her gaze watery. Guilt knifed me in the ribs, just below my heart.

"Sweet Zanna," she sighed. "Of course. Try and convince her to come. I'll see you at home."

Will waited until Grandmother had walked far enough away before coolly asking, "We're not going to June Street, are we?"

I stepped out of the flow of mourners and back toward another, older headstone.

"No. The man who's been following me is here. He's been watching the whole burial like it's some kind of show," I whispered. "I want to talk to him."

Will sucked in air. "What man? Someone's been following you?"

I filled him in as I wove my way through the headstones, taking a meandering path toward the tree where I'd seen the man.

"Zanna, stop." Will grabbed my arm and pulled me to a halt. "Adele had a strange man come up to her after the second warehouse fire, and you have a strange man following you now. Do you think this man could be one and the same?"

I hadn't thought that at all, actually. Adele hadn't had anyone following her, and Grandmother knew my stranger.

"I don't think so, Will," I said after a moment's contemplation.

"But you still want to talk to him? Zanna, that's not —" Will stopped his protest mid-sentence as the stranger stepped out from behind a massive headstone. He stood before us, calm and collected.

"You are correct, young man," the stranger said. "It's not the best idea for Miss Snow to be speaking with me right here, right now, what with all of these police officers swarming about."

But a fast glance behind us showed that most of the mourners, officers and all, were filing out through the gates, far away from this older section of the cemetery. The three of us were very much alone.

"And why don't you want the police to see you?" Will asked. But I already knew.

"Because he's a criminal," I answered. "My grandmother told me that he's a scoundrel of the worst sort."

And here I was insisting on speaking to him. It was madness, I knew, but it couldn't be helped.

My accusation brought a shine to the man's eyes

and a grin to his lips. That smile . . . it wasn't a sarcastic smile. It was real. Genuine. I knew I'd seen it somewhere before.

"You are also correct," he said, pulling on the brim of his hat. He kept his gaze locked with mine, his expression all humor. Mine was all mock bravery.

"My name is Matthew Leighton. To be specific, I am a thief. And even more specifically" — he arched an eyebrow — "I am your grandfather."

Chapter Ten

• • •

Detective Rule: Always keep the element of surprise within your control.

• • •

"YOU ARE NOT," I WHISPERED. "BOTH OF MY grandfathers are dead."

Will had gone stone-still beside me. This man was lying. He had to be. But he'd said his name was Leighton. *My* middle name was Leighton.

"You . . . you somehow found out what my middle name is and you're tricking me," I said.

"Why would I wish to do that?" he asked earnestly.

I searched for an answer, the sound of carriages pulling away from the cemetery and the chirps of birds in the branches above the only noises to be heard.

"So that I won't be afraid of you." It ended up sounding like a question.

He smiled again. "Unless you are a rare work of art hanging neglected on a wall somewhere, you have no reason at all to be afraid of me."

He took a step closer and shoved up the brim of his hat so I could see his eyes more clearly. They pulled me in. When I let myself stare into them, I saw something I didn't want to see.

My mother.

"Cecilia and Benjamin haven't told you about me, and I'm not surprised. I'm the reason they were forced out of Boston," he said. "The reason they've stayed away all this time."

I shook my head because it was all I could manage. This man, this self-proclaimed thief, was my grand-father? My parents had lied to me?

"When I heard you were coming to visit with Benjamin's mother, I . . ." He sighed and twirled the end of his walking cane into the air. "I couldn't stay away. I had to see the granddaughter I'd never had the chance to meet."

It was all too much to take in. I didn't want to believe it. And who had told him I was coming?

"So you're the one who's been stealing the art from the Horne warehouses," Will said when I couldn't open my mouth.

Matthew Leighton grimaced. "I can see how it might appear that way. I am a thief after all, and an art thief at that. But arson is not my modus operandi — it's simply not the way I work. I am not the one stealing the Horne collection."

His chin. The pointed, bottom-of-a-heart shape to it ... my mother had the same chin. The same genuine smile and dark gray eyes. But I wanted more proof than just a similar geography of the face.

"Why should we believe anything you say?" I asked. He twirled his cane around once again. He looked dashing and intellectual, and the sharp edge to his words, the perfect enunciation, told me he had a quick mind.

"I don't have any proof to hand you at the moment," he said. "And if I presented you with anything less than solid evidence, you would surely dismiss it. If you want answers you can trust, don't go to your grandmother. She's too stubborn. Bruce is more likely to tell you everything if you push him far enough."

I found myself nodding obediently and stopped. As if I was going to take advice from him!

"I'll find the answers my own way, thank you," I said.

Leighton tugged the brim of his hat down and bit back an amused grin.

"Of course you will," he replied, and turned to walk deeper into the cemetery. He looked over his shoulder as he walked away. "Take care, Suzanna. And try not to get into too much trouble, will you?"

He slipped behind another grand headstone and promptly disappeared.

•   •   •

We found Adele at her house. Apparently, following Dr. Philbrick hadn't proved dangerous — or valuable. It didn't matter. By the time Will and I reached June Street, my anxiety had found a new topic on which to dwell: Matthew Leighton.

Adele refused to come with us to the funeral reception. Will and I sat in her father's library for a good ten minutes trying to convince her, but she detested the customary reception after a funeral almost as much as the funeral itself, she said. At her mother's, she had endured countless sympathetic hugs and pats on the cheek, and promises of "life going on" and "all that rubbish," as Adele had called it.

I'd considered telling Adele about my encounter with Matthew Leighton, but every time I almost opened my mouth to do it, I stopped. He was an *art thief.* How could I admit I might have found the person stealing her father's collection, and that he claimed to be my grandfather? So Will and I eventually left for Grandmother's without a word of it. Carriages, buggies, and even a few motorcars lined each side of the street. Grandmother's brownstone seemed to be sucking in and belching out mourners clad in black and brown.

"Thanks for not telling Adele about what happened in the cemetery," I said to Will. We'd hardly spoken the whole way back to Knight Street. Will had seemed to know to stay mum about the grandfather/art thief topic, at least while my head was still spinning with the news.

"Are you going to ask your uncle about Matthew Leighton?" Will asked.

I knew I needed to, and as soon as possible. But what was I thinking? Uncle Bruce wasn't going to speak to me unless . . . well, unless I did as Leighton had said and *pushed him* to.

I needed to use the element of surprise.

Chapter Eleven

• • •

Sat., Sept. 26, 6:30 p.m.: Sitting inside Uncle Bruce's carriage, waiting for him to exit funeral reception. Planning ambush. Hoping he doesn't startle easily . . . and that he isn't armed.

• • •

THE DRIVER SHOOK THE CARRIAGE AS HE GOT up out of the box, and I shoved my pencil, notebook, and pocket watch into my cloak pocket. The inside of Uncle Bruce's carriage was so dark I'd barely been able to see what I was writing. The early dusk and pulled curtains added to the gloom.

Will had successfully diverted Uncle Bruce's driver's attention with false concerns over the lead mare's front leg, and I'd been able to slip inside the carriage to await my uncle's return. It had been nearly a half an hour since.

"Good evening, Detective," the driver called. It was finally time. "Are we waiting for Mrs. Snow?"

My uncle's answer came out gruff and weary. "No, she's staying with Mrs. Grogan tonight."

148

The door opened. Uncle Bruce shook the carriage as he climbed in.

"To the Copley," he directed.

I was in the seat opposite Uncle Bruce, and apparently drenched in shadows. He didn't see me until the driver had slammed the door.

"Who the —" Uncle Bruce slid forward onto the edge of his seat, looking ready to pounce.

"It's just me!" I cried. "Zanna!"

He sighed and fell back into his seat again. "What the blazes are you doing in my carriage, Suzanna? I could have shot you!"

He tucked his hand into his coat and I heard the distinct sound of steel coming to rest inside a hard leather holster. So he *had* been armed.

"I need to ask you some questions," I said as the horses pulled away from the curb and into the street.

Uncle Bruce twisted in his seat, preparing to shout for his driver to halt.

"Please, it's important!" I quickly said. "It's about Matthew Leighton."

Uncle Bruce stared back at me, his shout dying on his lips.

"How do you know that name?" he whispered instead.

I had him. The element of surprise was mine. I took an extra moment to revel in it.

"Is he really a thief?" I asked.

Uncle Bruce struck a match and lit the carriage lantern beside him. The red chimney glass bathed his face in a menacing light, shadowing the deep creases between his eyebrows.

"Yes."

I took a trembling breath. "Is he really my grandfather?"

Uncle Bruce's shoulders dropped. He sagged back in his seat. I smelled the cigar smoke and brandy he'd been indulging in all afternoon to numb the pain from his loss. The smell somehow made him seem old and powerless. His palm swept slowly across his forehead, a tired gesture to match his tired appearance.

"How do you know about him?" he finally asked. It wasn't a straight answer, but an answer nonetheless. Matthew Leighton *was* my grandfather.

"Why did everyone lie to me?"

Uncle Bruce suddenly leaned forward. "Because he is a thief!" The whites of his bulging eyes looked pink in the red lamplight. "And not just any small-time pickpocket, Suzanna. He's one of Boston's most wanted."

Those last few words shook me more deeply than the clattering wheels of the carriage. My own grandfather —

my mother's father — was a criminal. How could it be? For a detective-in-training, this was a scandal. I looked my uncle in the eye, realizing that for a seasoned, well-known detective like Bruce Snow, it was more than a scandal. It was a travesty.

"No one knows you're related to him," I whispered.

I recalled how he and Grandmother had both looked terrified when I'd almost announced my middle name was Leighton.

"No," he replied. "And no one ever can, Suzanna."

"But why?"

A small, humorless laugh erupted from Uncle Bruce's throat.

"I suppose I'm the one who has to tell you now," he said with evident resentment. "Matthew Leighton was the mastermind behind the very first case I investigated thirteen years ago — the Red Herring Heists."

I held my breath. Detective Grogan had told me a little about the unsolved case. To know that my own grandfather had been the mastermind behind it brought it much closer. I nearly felt guilty by association.

"Leighton left small clues to his identity at each crime scene, which we, of course, would then follow. Each time, the clue took us to nothing but a dead end. We soon realized they were red herrings, planted clues to lead us astray. To confuse the investigation," Uncle

Bruce explained. He'd never explained anything to me before. Right then my mind was torn between paying attention to what he was saying and the wonder of being in a true conversation with him.

"But then he got sloppy — as criminals always do," Uncle Bruce said darkly. "He made a trade on the underground market that one of our plainclothes traced back to him. We surrounded the building he lived in, and I went in first — it was to be my first big arrest, done single-handedly. But in addition to finding Leighton in his apartment, I also found a young woman I knew well: Cecilia Crocker, my brother's fiancée."

My heart skipped at the mention of my mother. It nearly stopped at what Uncle Bruce said next.

"She knew what he was. Not that he was the one behind the Red Herring Heists, but she knew her father was a thief. It was the reason she'd taken a different last name years before — to set herself apart should he ever be caught."

The horses whinnied and slapped at the pavement with their shod hooves as the carriage slowed. We must have been nearing the Copley. Uncle Bruce was too wrapped up in his story to notice or care.

"I had but a minute or two to make a decision. I could arrest her father, expose her as a criminal's daughter, taint my family name along with her own. Or I could let him go, granted that he disappear from Boston for good. Cecilia demanded he give us both his word." Uncle Bruce set his jaw and looked me in the eye. "He did. And I let them go."

We stared at each other in silence. My mother had known her father was a criminal. She'd *known*.

"You undermined an investigation," I said softly. "You jeopardized your career."

"I had to . . . for Cecilia." He twitched his mustache and cleared his throat. "Can you picture the headlines had I arrested her father?" He stretched his hands out into the air for emphasis as he mocked the imagined headline: " 'Red Herring Heists Detective Soon Related to Culprit.' I would have been a laughingstock."

And he would have never grown to be the revered detective he was today. The best in Boston.

"How did they get out of the apartment building without getting caught?" I asked.

He shifted uncomfortably in his seat. "I distracted the other officers with a false chase toward another exit. Leighton was good to his word: He disappeared. Cecilia and Benny married and left for Canada, wary that perhaps Leighton would return and try to contact them. Or that someone Cecilia knew would somehow connect her to Leighton."

My fingers ached from being clenched for so long. I uncurled each one, thinking of all the lies I'd grown up believing. Of the secret way my mother had given me a sliver of the truth through my middle name. She'd named me after her father — a thief she must have continued to love, despite his faults.

Uncle Bruce sat forward. "Now it's your turn to explain how you learned about Matthew Leighton."

Uncle Bruce had been honest with me, and so I'd be honest with him.

"He's been following me around Boston."

He sat back, startled. "*What?*"

"And I spoke to him today after the funeral," I said. "In the cemetery. He told me who he was, but I didn't believe him. He said you'd tell me the truth."

I still couldn't believe Uncle Bruce had actually told me all of this. Then again, he'd been holding the truth in for a very long time. It had to have been weighing on him.

"Are you telling me that Matthew Leighton is in Boston?" he asked, sobering up from his state of shock. He didn't give me a chance to respond.

"Xavier Horne's artwork. All those places destroyed, the art supposedly lost . . . stolen from the Philbrick home . . ." He trailed off, sounding like he was latching on to Adele's previously dismissed theory. And then he recalled something else: *"The red herrings have returned. So it was him."*

"But he isn't the one stealing the Horne collection," I said. "He said it was someone else. That he was trying to find proof to present to me."

Uncle Bruce snorted as the carriage came to a halt. "Of course he'd tell you that. But think like a detective for a minute, Suzanna, and you'll notice the connection between this and the Red Herring Heists. The warehouse fires are what?"

I expected him to answer his own question, but he didn't. He was actually waiting for me to answer it. My mind worked furiously.

"The warehouse fires are . . ." I felt hopeless for a moment. And then it struck me. "Red herrings. They're *giant* red herrings."

He smiled and nodded, pleased. I wanted to be pleased as well, but if this was true, then that meant my grandfather had been lying to me.

I hated being lied to.

"Do you know where he's living? Did he say anything at all to you about where you could find him?" Uncle Bruce asked from the edge of his seat.

I answered no but that perhaps he'd continue to follow me. Uncle Bruce burst into action, practically kicking open the carriage door. His driver, who had been about to open the door, leaped out of the way. Uncle Bruce jumped to the curb below.

"Return my niece to Knight Street," he ordered the startled driver. "We'll go to the station as soon as you get back."

Uncle Bruce started to close the door, but stopped.

"It would be best, Suzanna" — he leaned in and lowered his voice — "if you didn't mention Leighton in front of my mother. He isn't a topic she fares well with."

Uncle Bruce shut the door, and the driver cracked the reins. I jerked forward and then back again, slamming against the high cushion behind me. He was right, of course. I'd already seen Grandmother's reaction to Matthew Leighton once before. She'd called him a scoundrel of the worst sort.

But what if Leighton wasn't the thief this time? Uncle Bruce had said he'd been good to his word. He'd stayed out of sight for thirteen years. Why would he decide to break that promise now? And to burn down Detective Grogan's home — to kill him. It didn't make sense.

I rode back to Grandmother's house, knowing I should have been writing everything down in my notebook before the details got fuzzy. But writing it would have made it real.

I didn't want any of it to be real.

Chapter Twelve

• • •

Sun., Sept. 27, 8 a.m.: Bad feeling brewing in stomach. Leighton is a thief, but not an arsonist. Not his "modus operandi." Suspect Uncle Bruce is wrong — again.

• • •

MARGARET MARY HUMMED AT THE STOVE while flipping thick strips of bacon in a cast-iron pan. I'd looked forward to another Sunday breakfast all week. Margaret Mary made enough food to feed the entire Boston police department should they have all shown up at the door. But this morning, I could barely think about finishing the mug of hot chocolate in front of me, let alone the feast that she was busy preparing.

I'd been up for hours already, worrying and second-guessing. Uncle Bruce wanted to close this case more than anything and I'd practically handed Matthew Leighton over as a prime suspect. My own grandfather. Why would Uncle Bruce be fine with arresting him now if he hadn't wanted to thirteen years ago? My mother had changed her name twice now, had moved far away and severed all ties with her former life.

Perhaps she couldn't be reconnected to Leighton now, after all these years.

And back then the crime had only been stealing art. Arson and murder were crimes that Uncle Bruce could not turn his back on. Not even for family.

"Look lively, girl," Margaret Mary said as she came toward me with a spatula heaped with crisp bacon. She set the bacon on a plate before me. "Little something to hold you over. Now, what's this? The chocolate too rich for you this morning?"

I sighed into my mug.

"I'm sorry, I'm —"

The doorbell punctured the rest of my excuse. My pocket watch read five minutes past eight o'clock. Too early for visitors. Margaret Mary scowled, but I could tell she was happy for the chance to serve more than just Grandmother and me.

I got up, restless. "I'll go see who it is."

By the time I reached the foyer, Bertie had already answered the door and de-cloaked Grandmother's early morning guest: Uncle Bruce.

"She's in the kitchen, I believe," Bertie was saying to him. Uncle Bruce started for the front receiving room but pulled up short when he saw me in the back of the front hallway near the kitchen door.

158

"Just the girl I needed to see," he said, pursing his lips. It wasn't a frown, though. He looked purposeful, as if he was on a mission.

"Me?" I asked.

"We have work to see to, Suzanna. The department needs your help this morning." He was already reaching for his coat and hat.

My help? The department — the Boston police needed me? The words sounded so glorious I wanted him to say them again.

"Tell my mother Suzanna has come with me on an errand," he instructed Bertie, who stood by the front door, clearly perplexed by the whirlwind visit. "I hope to have her back in time for luncheon."

Bertie rushed to take down my cloak.

"But where are we going?" I asked.

Uncle Bruce opened the front door, letting in a brisk morning breeze. "To Boston Common."

I followed him out to the waiting carriage and climbed in. There, seated on a bench, was Will.

"What are you doing here?" I asked, sitting beside him. He wore a dark expression.

"You're not going to like this, Zanna, but —" He bit off the rest of his explanation as Uncle Bruce climbed in and pounded on the roof to signal the driver.

I turned to Uncle Bruce, thoroughly confused now. "Why do you need me on Boston Common?"

I reached for my notebook, but realized it was still on Margaret Mary's kitchen table. *Blast.*

Uncle Bruce smoothed down his black mustache. "You're going to help the police obtain a criminal today, Suzanna."

I straightened my spine, startled. "How do you mean?"

He smoothed down his mustache again. I wondered if that was one of Uncle Bruce's nervous tics. Will would know. I glanced out the corner of my eye at him. He still looked cross. Uncle Bruce spoke, and when he did, I pieced together that Will must already know about the Snow family secret.

"I gave him a chance once. A chance to go straight. I thought he'd made use of it. But it seems once a thief, always a thief." Uncle Bruce's dark eyes flashed with anger. "Now I realize he is more dangerous than I thought. There are some things that are more important than my reputation. My partner deserves justice."

I shook my head, still not understanding what it was he wanted me to do on Boston Common.

"It's not justice to arrest the wrong man," I said. "I don't think he's the one behind the fires or thefts. There's a framer on Varden Street called Mr. Dashner —"

Uncle Bruce set his jaw. "I know Dashner. What of him?"

The carriage turned a corner sharply and I bumped into Will.

"Dashner would know the exact dimensions of the frames for each artwork," Will said, his glower still in place.

"If he wanted to, he could have crafted replica frames of the artwork stored in Mr. Horne's ware-houses," I added.

"He had close contact with Mr. Horne," Will threw in. "He could have memorized the safe-box combinations when he exchanged the stored art for the display art inside Mr. Horne's home."

We spewed out our facts to match the speed of the rattling carriage, including how Mr. Dashner was on a curious holiday at the moment. Neither of us made mention of the rare Degas statue, but I couldn't help but think it was in danger as well. Uncle Bruce listened to it all without interrupting. And after we finished, he continued to remain quiet as he stared out the window.

"We have no evidence at all against Jonathan Dashner," he finally said.

"There is no evidence against Matthew Leighton, either," I shot back.

The carriage slowed, but looking outside I didn't see the trees of Boston Common, just rows of buildings on each side of the street.

"He was fingered for the Red Herring Heists thirteen years ago," Uncle Bruce said, his temper rising. "With the similarities between the two cases, it is all we need to make an arrest."

The driver came down from the box and opened the door. Uncle Bruce didn't move to get out.

"Are you ready to work for the Boston police?" he asked me, then looked to Will as well. My palms began to sweat inside my gloves.

"Yes," I answered. "But —"

"Good. You two will leave from here to take a stroll through Boston Common."

Uncle Bruce made room for me to exit. That was it?

"We're just . . . taking a walk?" I asked. There had to be more to the plan than that.

"The rest will be handled by more experienced members of my department," he replied. "You will simply walk until you are signaled to return to the carriage."

I exhaled, the wind having been sucked from my wings. What kind of police work was that? I met Will's dark eyes and saw impatience there. He wasn't very good at hiding his anxiety. He had something more to tell me.

I hopped down to the curb. Will followed. With a tip of his brimmed hat, Uncle Bruce drew back inside the carriage and shut the door. Will took my elbow and started off down the sidewalk.

"What's really going on?" I asked.

Practically glued to my side, his hand still tight around my elbow, Will answered, "Nothing you're going to like, that's for sure."

I glanced over my shoulder, back at my uncle's carriage. "I know he wants to arrest my grandfather."

Will and I turned the corner onto the next block of buildings. We'd parked far from the Common.

"But why are we strolling through a park?" I asked.

Will let go of my arm at last. He swiped off his cap and took a nervous look up and down the street.

"Because you're the bait," he answered.

Bait! So I wasn't doing police work after all. Uncle Bruce had been patronizing me the whole time. I clenched my hands into fists. I should have known.

"What makes him think my grandfather will approach me on Boston Common?" The trees and lawns of the Common came into view beyond a neat row of brownstones.

"I don't know that part," Will admitted. "Uncle Bruce didn't think I *needed* to know. Big surprise there."

We waited for a trolley car to rattle by on a set of steel tracks, and then crossed toward the park entrance.

A man seated on a nearby bench lifted his gaze from his newspaper and made eye contact with me. It lasted a few seconds too long. Will guided me past him and onto a set of stone steps that led down to the grassy lawns.

"That man back there," Will whispered, still stuck to my side. "I've seen him before. He works with Uncle Bruce. Another detective on the force."

As soon as Will confirmed my suspicion, I spotted three more men within sight. One feeding ducks, another pretending to sketch something while leaning against a tree, and the third smoking a pipe on a park bench.

"The fools. They might as well pin their badges to their foreheads," I hissed. "As if Matthew Leighton would come within a hundred yards of me when the police are lurking about."

And who was to say he was even here watching? We'd finally met face-to-face the day before. He might not feel the need to follow me again.

"Well, Uncle Bruce is counting on him being here, watching you," Will replied. "And I'm just supposed to stroll you through the park until he shows himself. He's already met me. . . . I think Uncle Bruce is hoping your grandfather doesn't see me as a threat."

There were scores of people strolling through the Common this morning. Men and women, arm in arm, children dressed in their Sunday finest, nannies pushing prams along the brick walk that wound throughout the park, a grouping of older ladies settled on a bench underneath the limbs of a maple tree. And, of course, plainclothes policemen. But I didn't see my grandfather anywhere.

"He won't come near me," I said again as Will and I curved around a small fountain. I hated that I was being used as "bait," as Will had called it. Nothing more than a worm pinned to a hook, cast out to lure in my uncle's prime suspect.

"What do you think?" I asked.

"About what?"

"My grandfather. Do you think he's guilty?"

Will tucked his chin toward his chest and exhaled loudly. He shoved his hands deep into his pockets and came to a standstill beside the bubbling stone fountain.

"Zanna, he's guilty of something one way or

another." His honesty stung. "But I think our uncle has a target and he can't see beyond it."

I defied my orders to keep walking and sat on the edge of the fountain. The stone was cold, not yet warmed by the morning sun.

"That's what I think, too," I said.

Just then, a man in a rumpled coat and crushed hat stepped up behind Will and shoved him forward.

"What do you think you're —" Will started to say. But the man took a swift jab to Will's jaw. I leaped from the fountain just as Will went stumbling, stunned by the unexpected blow.

"What are you doing?" I yelled at the man as I reached for Will, who lay on his side at the base of the fountain. The man grabbed hold of my wrist and jerked me away.

Alarmed, I finally stopped to take a good look at his face. He wore beggar's clothing, but his face was shaved smooth and he smelled of talc and cologne. Beggars didn't wear cologne.

"Who are you?" I asked. The man started away from the fountain, dragging me with him.

"Hey!" I heard Will shout from behind me. When I craned my neck back, I saw two other men crouched over him. They were blocking Will from getting up and pursuing the beggar and me. And they were both my uncle's policemen.

You're the bait, Will had said. What would draw my grandfather out from his hiding spot amongst the Common's trees or monuments? A rogue man threatening to harm me, that's what. This man wasn't a beggar — he was a policeman! And if he was indeed here, my grandfather might reveal himself any second now to come to my rescue.

I hadn't wanted my uncle to arrest my grandfather in the first place, and I certainly didn't want to aid him by playing the damsel in distress. I had to do something.

I brought the plainclothes policeman's hand to my mouth and sunk my teeth into his skin. He released me with a yowl, and I kicked him in the shin. I then darted in the opposite direction, up a knoll toward a small bridge that ran across a pond.

If I could prove to my grandfather that I could escape on my own, perhaps he wouldn't come out of hiding. I remembered the time he'd come running across the back courtyard of the academy when I'd been dangling from the fire ladder, and I ran faster toward the bridge. But at the top of the knoll, I heard the huffing of the injured policeman climbing up after me.

There was a slight dip of the land after the crest of the knoll and I hurried down it. But I couldn't go across the bridge — I needed to get out of sight, fast. Oh, how furious Uncle Bruce was going to be!

I spotted my perfect hideaway: underneath the bridge along the banking of the pond. I slipped down and scooted under, heart hammering inside my chest.

"It seems great minds do think alike."

I clamped down on my scream and wheeled around. Matthew Leighton was behind me, crouched in the narrow space between the muddy banking and the cross-beams of the bridge.

"Or perhaps the adage should be *desperate* minds think alike," he said.

"You can't be here!" I hissed. He only grinned.

"I realized that, once I'd entered the park and saw Bruce's minions scattered about. So much for my hoping you and your friend were taking an innocent stroll," he whispered. "I'd wanted to see how you were dealing with —" He stopped and pressed a finger to his lips. The pounding of feet on the knoll behind us sent my stomach up into my throat. I crouched even lower, but my boots and the hem of my dress and cloak were already submerged in the soft, wet banking.

"This way, come on!" someone yelled, and then the pounding feet carried off into the opposite direction. They weren't going to cross the bridge, thank heavens.

"— how you were coping with everything I told you yesterday," he finished.

It didn't matter how I was coping, not right then at least. "My uncle wants to arrest you for the Horne fires and art thefts."

"That's hardly a surprise," Leighton replied. He looked unperturbed as he crouched in our cramped hiding spot, his arms wrapped around his legs. "I take it you do not agree with his verdict?"

I hesitated, but then shook my head. "No. I don't think you've stolen anything."

His blithe expression shifted to something darker. "Don't exonerate me just yet, Suzanna. I *have* stolen. Just not from Xavier Horne."

I lifted my chin. "You seem very proud to be a thief."

"I won't pretend to be something I'm not," he replied.

The echoes of more shouts drifted under the bridge.

"You have to go," I said.

Leighton took a few froglike jumps forward until he was right beside me. "Your uncle turned me loose much the same way once. I hope this doesn't mean you'll grow to be the same kind of detective he is."

He might have been my grandfather, but he was also infuriating and arrogant.

"I'm not turning you loose completely. You said you know who the real thief is. Is it Mr. Dashner, the framer on Varden Street?"

He removed his domelike black hat and peered at me. "Dashner? Why would you suspect him?"

"Because he knows everything there is to know about Mr. Horne's paintings and frames, including how to craft replicas if he wanted to."

My grandfather took another crouching leap toward me. I noticed he had a sharp kind of smell to him. Not anything unpleasant. No, he smelled like . . . soap. A musky, woodland scent.

"It's not Dashner," he said with conviction. Enough conviction to make me believe it, too.

Just then, another burst of shouting came from close by.

"I hate to cut our conversation short, but my window of opportunity for escape is growing drastically smaller," Leighton said, and prepared to dart up the bank. He tipped his hat toward me. "I'm indebted to your efforts today, Suzanna. It seems it wasn't my time to go to prison after all."

And with that, he fled up the bank. I waited for my uncle's officers to spot him and give chase. But after a full minute of silence had passed, I exhaled and relaxed. He'd slipped away unseen.

I emerged from underneath the bridge, the wet, weedy land sucking at my boots as I tried to climb back up the bank. I wanted to slip away unseen, too. Unfortunately, I had to face Uncle Bruce and his police officers, including the one I'd bitten.

"Now or never," I grumbled, and made my way toward the knoll.

Chapter Thirteen

• • •

Detective Rule: Lying is wrong. However, weaving an intricate excuse in a time of need is oftentimes acceptable.

• • •

"HOW WAS I SUPPOSED TO KNOW THE BEGGAR was actually a police officer?" I wailed to Grandmother. She sat beside me on the parlor sofa, her soft, wrinkled hands clasping my own.

Uncle Bruce paced the length of the room. His usually glossed-back hair fell in wild pieces around his forehead.

"I explained that you'd be working covertly," he said.

"You didn't say I'd be attacked!" I put on the best expression of alarm I could muster. It worked on Grandmother at least.

"Bruce, how could you? Using a young girl for your own ends . . . it's despicable. And to have your man punch dear Will in the jaw!"

Grandmother settled in closer to me. Her chin quivered with fury. Will's lip had been split, but otherwise he was fine — other than the rash of foul language that had erupted from his mouth when he'd next seen his uncle.

Uncle Bruce swung out his arm as if orating to a massive audience. "It was an operation of the utmost importance, Mother! If a bruised jaw and a frightened girl were the only casualties of apprehending Matthew Leighton, then it would have been worth it!"

Grandmother's back stiffened. "You have gone too far, Bruce. *Too far.*"

She let go of my hand and stood. "You will apologize to Will's mother for the injury he received today. You should also apologize to Will — *and* Suzanna."

Despite his age, his mother's scolding made Uncle Bruce look like a petulant young boy.

"I'll leave you to it," Grandmother said, and then swept out of the parlor. Uncle Bruce pinned me with a dark stare.

"You deliberately let him go, didn't you?" he asked.

I got up from the sofa. "He knows who the real thief is."

Uncle Bruce snorted, muttering sarcastically, "Of course he does."

He picked up his pacing once more. The planned sting had gone down horribly — bested by a little girl. Uncle Bruce had looked like a fool in front of his men.

Perhaps if he hadn't been letting anger and revenge drive his operation, it would have succeeded.

"He might be able to help if you'd let him," I said. Uncle Bruce flushed to the roots of his hair.

"I do not work with criminals. And if you entertain dreams of being a detective someday, then you will follow that same rule."

He stormed from the parlor.

If only Uncle Bruce would open up his eyes and mind. Who better to catch an art thief than a thief cut from the same cloth?

• • •

Monday morning a cold rain drummed the top of Grandmother's carriage as we rode to the academy together. I'd told her I hadn't minded walking the few blocks, but she'd insisted on the carriage and on coming with me. The fires, my uncle's shenanigans, and Detective Grogan's death had rattled her more than she was willing to admit.

I sat with my notebook open on my lap, reading through all the pages I'd filled in since arriving in Boston. Had it really only been two weeks ago? I felt like I'd been there much longer than that.

"Zanna, I think it would be best if I sent a telegram

to your parents," Grandmother said. We'd been sitting in silence ever since leaving the brownstone.

My pointer finger streaked to a stop underneath a sentence I'd been reading. I glanced up at her. "I just sent them a reply to their last telegram a few days ago."

Grandmother shook her head. "I mean, I think it would be best if I sent word that you're coming home earlier than planned."

I slapped the notebook shut. "What? No! I can't go back to Loch Harbor, not yet. Grandmother, please."

How could I explain how badly I needed to stay in Boston? Adele and Will . . . they were counting on me. My grandfather was counting on me, even if he didn't quite know it yet.

"I have a feeling your desire to stay has nothing to do with how much you're enjoying Miss Doucette's academy?" Grandmother asked with a sly lift of her brow.

I had the grace to look a little sheepish and shook my head. "It's not the academy. It's this case, Grandmother. It's . . . it's something I've started and I want to finish it. I *need* to finish it."

She fiddled with her hands, dressed in black lace gloves. Perhaps she'd imagined I wanted to stay for deeper reasons, like getting to know her better. I suddenly felt so single-minded. Really, how much time had I spent with my grandmother? Not much. I'd been too wrapped up in the Horne case.

"Maybe . . . you could help me?" I said in a small, questioning voice.

She stilled her fidgeting hands. "Me? Why, I don't know how I could help."

"You could tell me what you know about Matthew Leighton." I knew it was a risk. Uncle Bruce had advised me not to say a word about him, and her spell the evening of the museum concert had given me a fright. But she knew him better than I did. She might have information I could use.

Grandmother's reaction was immediate. She tightened her small shoulders, and her blue eyes hardened over with what seemed like a layer of frost.

"The only thing I know about that man is that he is a disgrace. He's an unlawful, self-serving rogue, and the people who are tied to him — whether they want to be or not — suffer because of it."

My mother must have suffered most of all. How had she handled it when she'd learned what he did for a living? She was so proper and kind and graceful. How could her father be so different from her?

"I know he's a thief, and I know I've only met him a few times." My thumb fanned the pages of my notebook as I thought. "But he didn't strike me as the sort of person who would burn down buildings and put people in harm's way."

He'd even stayed by Grandmother's side after she'd fainted at the museum — until people started coming toward us. Grandmother despised him, so I was expecting her to reply with a hearty reassurance that he was indeed the sort of person to do those deeds. But instead, she inhaled deeply and held the breath in her lungs a long moment. Thinking.

She exhaled. "No, he doesn't, does he? He is a crafty old crook, but nothing more depraved than that."

She glanced at the edge of the notebook I was absentmindedly fanning the pages of. "What do you have in there about him?"

I stilled my thumb. "How do you know I have anything at all?" Grandmother hadn't ever asked me what my notebook was for, and I hadn't offered the information.

She smiled. "You forget, Bruce used to keep notebooks filled with his case studies, too."

Yes, I had forgotten. Detective Grogan had mentioned the notebooks the day I'd arrived at the brownstone, as well as something else. *"I might have discovered some similarities between the Horne fires and an older case, one that Bruce worked on when he was a rookie."*

Had he been referring to the Red Herring Heists? If Detective Grogan had found a connection and had managed to find proof . . . well, it would be a solid motive for the Red Herring mastermind to want to shut him up for good. With a sinking chill, I flipped through the pages of the notebook until I landed on the entry about the strange man who had first suggested to Adele that her father's precious art was being stolen.

"*Odd smell*," I read aloud, though mostly to myself. "*Soap. Musky. Like wood.*" My finger stalled underneath that last word. I looked up from the notebook. "Like wood."

"What's that, dear?" Grandmother asked. "Who has an odd smell?"

The day before, beneath the bridge on Boston Common, my grandfather had had a clean, soapy scent, too, and it had been musky. I remembered thinking it was like a pine tree or balsam. A Christmas smell.

"Matthew Leighton," I answered my grandmother, though my mind was already charging ahead.

Could Adele's strange man and my grandfather be one and the same? Will had suggested it at Detective Grogan's burial, but I'd shrugged off the suspicion. Now I wasn't so sure. If my grandfather had been the one to tell Adele about the art thefts, he most definitely couldn't be guilty. Why draw attention to the stolen art if he was the one swiping it? I had to tell my uncle. I closed the book, disheartened. As if he'd ever listen to a word I had to say again. I'd thwarted his attempt at capturing Matthew Leighton. I was sure I'd never be forgiven.

"Well, I'm not sure how he smells is going to help with an investigation," Grandmother said with a sigh. "But I can understand your wanting to stay and see things through. It's very . . . responsible of you, Suzanna. If you wish to stay in Boston, I suppose you may. But I warn you: If your investigating in any way turns hazardous" — Grandmother shook a finger toward me — "I want you to promise me you'll ask me for help. Is that understood?"

The carriage arrived outside the academy. I stared at my grandmother, dumbfounded. She hadn't demanded I *stop* investigating should it turn hazardous?

"Well?" she pressed. "Do I have your word?"

"Y-yes," I stammered. "Yes, of course."

She nodded. "Very well, then. Off you go."

I fumbled putting away my notebook and gathering my books, and, still dazed, got out of the carriage. Grandmother gave me a prim wave through the window after the driver closed it. I waved back, still shocked. My grandmother was to be my new ally? I turned to go inside the academy, wondering if the day could possibly turn any more bizarre.

• • •

The morning slugged forward, the clocks stuck in what felt like a timeless abyss. In contrast to stolen masterpieces, fiery blazes, and secret identities, the needlepoint, watercolors, and posture exercises Adele and I were subjected to seemed more like weapons of torture.

It wasn't until our early afternoon constitutional stroll that I had the chance to talk to Adele privately. I wanted to ask her to make a run past Mr. Dashner's frame shop again after dismissal with me. We paired off from the other girls in the academy courtyard. Our shoulders brushed against each other and she gave me a nudge.

"How did you manage it, Zanna?"

"Manage what?" I asked. She nudged me again, knocking me off balance and closer to the rim of the stone fountain.

"Oh, stop! You know exactly what I mean. My father got a message last night from your uncle. How did you convince him that the art might be getting stolen? And do you know who the prime suspect is? My father said they already have one!"

I choked on a response. I didn't want to lie to Adele, but I also wasn't prepared to tell her about my grandfather. He was a thief. I felt a little like how my mother must have: I didn't want to be associated with something so low.

"I just told him about Mr. Dashner and the frames," I answered. Adele slowed her rotation of the fountain.

"But that was only speculation," she replied. "We never found any proof. You yourself said your uncle wouldn't listen to anything *but* proof."

I suddenly wished for a less astute partner. Because that's what she was, wasn't she? My partner. And I was hiding something from her.

"And what happened on the Common yesterday?" Adele asked. "My father said they nearly nabbed the suspect, and that you were there. You and Will."

Saying I'd been used as bait would only lead Adele to ask why I might have successfully drawn the suspect out into the open in the first place. But saying my uncle had simply asked me to be there during a sting would have been an outright lie. Adele would never have believed it anyway. I groped for something to say, but came up blank.

Adele stopped walking. "What aren't you telling me?"

I unbuttoned the top clasp of my cloak, hot with nerves. "I wish I could tell you, Adele, but I ... I can't."

The frigid glare she'd hit me with my first few days at the academy returned full force. "Can't or won't? I thought we were investigating together."

I took a step after her. "We are, but —"

Adele brushed past me. "I get it, Suzanna. Really, I do. You're just like your uncle and you don't even know it."

The insult hit like a brick. "My uncle?"

I ignored the girls around us, all stopping to watch our spat. Adele raised her voice just enough so that everyone could listen in easily.

"There's only room for one ego around here, isn't that right?"

Ego? I didn't have an out-of-control ego! I just had a gigantic secret.

"That's not it at all, Adele."

She charged past me again, heading back toward the academy doors. "You'll find an invitation to my house tonight when you get home. You can ignore it and tell your grandmother I've changed my mind."

Adele stormed inside, leaving me frazzled by the whirlwind of misunderstanding. I hadn't even been able to ask her to go with me to Varden Street. It looked like I was on my own after all, just as Adele assumed I wanted it.

Chapter Fourteen

• • •

Mon., Sept. 28, 3:30 p.m.: Mr. Dashner's frame shop finally open. Going in (before I lose what's left of my nerve).

• • •

I WASN'T THE ONLY PERSON INSIDE MR. Dashner's shop. Someone I presumed was Mr. Dashner himself and a uniformed police officer were standing in the back of the shop, engaged in a hushed discussion. Unfinished frames hung from pegs on the walls, cloth-draped paintings sat propped against one another on the floor, and a thick metal safe door built into one of the walls was propped open. I hovered near the front door, thinking to slip out quickly, when the officer lifted his head and made eye contact with me.

I hadn't seen this officer before, I didn't think. He didn't seem to recognize me, either, and went back to writing on a small pad of paper. Mr. Dashner gestured wildly with his hands — both of which were mottled by a bright red rash. He took notice of me.

"I'll be with you in a moment, miss," he said, and

then turned back to the officer, saying, "It was the only thing taken. I'm sure of it."

The officer nodded, finished writing, and closed up his notebook.

"I'll ask around. See if anyone saw something suspicious."

Mr. Dashner thanked him, but as he walked the officer to the door, he looked like he might faint. His skin had a yellow pallor and a sheen of sweat glistened on his forehead. And peeking out from his band collar was a rash of red boils.

"I'm sorry to keep you waiting," Mr. Dashner said to me once the officer had left. He pulled out a handkerchief and blotted at his forehead.

"Is everything all right?" I asked.

"No. I'm afraid it's not." He shuffled back toward the shop's work space, and leaned against the open safe door once he got there. "I'm ruined."

I walked after him. "Ruined? How do you mean?"

He closed the safe door and spun the dial. "I was robbed last night. Someone broke into my safe and took a painting that belongs to one of my most important clients."

The smell of glue, paint, and new wood suddenly made my stomach churn. I wanted to ask if the client was Xavier Horne, but couldn't. If it was, Mr. Dashner would question how I'd guessed right off the top of my head.

"Was it an expensive painting?" I asked instead.

Mr. Dashner rubbed his hands together fretfully, then scratched at the bumpy red rash covering them.

"Yes. Very. A Cézanne."

It *was* Mr. Horne's painting. Mr. Dashner had told the police officer that nothing else had been taken. So the Cézanne had been the sole object of desire. That painting was the only warehouse-stored artwork that had not been moved to either Dr. Philbrick's or Detective Grogan's homes — and now even that was gone. That meant five paintings had been stolen and eleven had been supposedly burned. Sixteen in all. *Sixteen.*

Perhaps being inside a frame shop made it easy for me to recall the significance of that number. Signor Periggi had constructed eleven frames for his client, but hadn't he said that the original order had been for sixteen? Without caring what Mr. Dashner might have thought of it, I brought out my notebook and flipped back to the page with Periggi's information. Yes, he'd said *sedici* — sixteen. So eleven frames constructed, and eleven paintings burned. Five frames canceled, and five paintings stolen instead of destroyed. And those five had been removed from the warehouses after the fires. After Periggi had received his original order for a full sixteen.

It wasn't a coincidence. I didn't believe in them. Had the thief hired Signor Periggi to reconstruct the frames, only to then change the order when it became clear they wouldn't be in the warehouses any longer? But then why had there only been cancellations for the Cézanne, and the four pieces brought to Dr. Philbrick's? Why hadn't there been a cancellation for the six destroyed in Detective Grogan's house fire? Why hadn't those other places — Dr. Philbrick's home and Mr. Dashner's shop — been set ablaze?

Mr. Dashner grimaced at his hands, still scratching.

"How did you get the rash?" I asked. He hadn't yet asked me what I wanted. I would take advantage of his distraction for as long as I could.

He held them up to inspect the angry red patches, then shoved them into his pockets.

"I've been away in the Berkshires on a fly-fishing trip. I had the misfortune of falling into a patch of poison ivy." He shook his head and then scratched at one of the many welts on his neck.

"I'm sorry," I said, more confused than before. How could he be the culprit if he hadn't even been in Boston? Unless he'd had a partner in crime.

"Forgive me," he said. "May I help you with something?"

I'd planned on using the "present for my grandmother" story again, but with this new development, I wasn't sure of the point. It seemed Mr. Dashner had indeed been on holiday, plagued by bad luck and poison ivy, and it did look like he was devastated by the theft.

"No, it's nothing. I can come back another time when things are more . . . settled," I said, backing up toward the door.

He didn't try to stop me. Instead, he mopped his face again with his handkerchief and mumbled to himself as I shut the door behind me. I walked back into the slanting rain to Grandmother's carriage. Mr. Dashner very well *could* have been filing a false theft report. He *could* have had a partner, allowing him to conveniently be in the Berkshires during the last fire. But if there was a connection to the order for sixteen frames from Signor Periggi, that put Mr. Dashner even farther down the possibilities list. Why would a framer hire another framer to construct decoy frames?

If it wasn't Dashner, then who was it? I didn't want to consider Matthew Leighton. Still, it couldn't be avoided.

I arrived back at 224 Knight Street and found

Grandmother eagerly waiting to tell me that I'd had two invitations arrive during the day. I already knew about the one from Adele. The other was an invitation to a last-minute bon voyage dinner for Hannah Grogan at the Copley Square Hotel that night.

"Bon voyage? Where is she going?" I gave the rectangular vellum card back to Grandmother as Bertie stripped off my cloak and brought it to dry by the hearth.

"She has family in Paris who want her to stay with them for the time being." Grandmother set the invitation on the mantel. "You're in high demand this evening, it seems. Tell me, which will it be, June Street or the Copley?"

I hadn't yet told Grandmother that Adele had *dis*-invited me. I sat heavily on the sofa. Grandmother misinterpreted it.

"I would imagine you'd rather avoid your uncle," she said, and took a seat beside me. "I don't mean to make excuses for his behavior yesterday, but Zanna, Bruce has never lost a partner before. We have to give him a little room for anger."

My blood hummed in my veins, ready to boil. "Even if that means letting him arrest the wrong person?"

He'd done it before, in Loch Harbor when he'd arrested my friend Isaac Quimby based on evidence that had obviously been planted. He'd do it again to close a case to his personal satisfaction. How many other cases had he closed this way? I didn't want to know.

"Matthew Leighton should not be here in Boston," Grandmother said, her voice terse. "He knew to stay away. It was part of their agreement."

"And he did stay away. He slipped off the face of the earth for thirteen years. What if he truly has kept his word? What if he makes an honest living now?"

Grandmother looked at me with plain-as-day pity. First, Adele had rejected me in front of the entire academy, and now Grandmother thought I was naive. I couldn't handle any more shame. I shot up from the sofa.

"Maybe I'll just stay here tonight," I said.

Grandmother followed me and got to her feet. "I didn't mean to upset you, Zanna. Oh, if only you'd never had to learn about Matthew Leighton at all! I just don't understand how he knew you were coming. It was as if he knew to expect you."

Grandmother's pale face had turned waxy. She took out her fan and beat the ruffles madly. Spotting the warning signs of another attack, I quickly worked to calm her.

"I'm not upset, Grandmother. I'm glad I know about him. Just like I'm glad I came to Boston."

I hoped it didn't sound like too much of a sugar coating. But I certainly didn't want Dr. Philbrick to pay us a visit today. I hadn't seen him since we'd bumped into each other outside Signor Periggi's frame shop. My worry for Grandmother came to a halt as I recalled how Dr. Philbrick's hand had reached out for the knob to Periggi's shop. Twice.

I'd passed it off as his being flustered over the memory of Detective Grogan's burned remains. Dr. Philbrick *was* an art collector, a friend of Mr. Horne's, and perhaps a patron of Periggi's. And not only had four of the (possibly) canceled frames been stolen from his house, but Periggi had said the person who'd ordered the frames had been extremely picky in his orders. Dr. Philbrick fit that bill nicely. Could he have ordered the custom frames?

The wind from Grandmother's beating fan brought me back to the parlor.

"Do you think maybe you could drop me off at Adele's tonight?"

I wasn't sure if going to Adele's was a good idea, but perhaps I could distract her with my half-formed theories about Dr. Philbrick. Adele *had* seemed suspicious of him to begin with.

Grandmother's fan slowed. "Of course. I'm sure Hannah will understand, and she won't want for dinner guests. Bruce, Katherine, Will, and a good number of the police force will be there. I daresay Boston will have to be on its best behavior tonight." She slid her ruffled fan shut. "The police will be quite distracted."

She stood up. "Be ready in an hour. And bring your needlepoint. Perhaps Adele can help you with your stitches."

She rang for Bertie and shuffled out of the front parlor. I'd make her happy and bring my sad-looking needlepoint. But with these new thoughts regarding Dr. Philbrick, I highly doubted Adele and I would be discussing stitches and thread tonight.

● ● ●

The carriage had barely stopped rolling up to the front steps of Adele's house when I leaped out and started to shut the door behind me.

"It's all right, Grandmother, I can go in alone. You'll be late for dinner as it is." I felt only slightly guilty that I'd dawdled getting ready just to be sure of it.

"I'll at least wait until the butler sees you in," she said. Perfect! This way she wouldn't witness Adele's sour expression when she saw that I'd arrived uninvited.

The butler opened the door and I gave Grandmother a pert wave. She waved back, but through the glass I thought I could see her pursed lips twitched to the side and one of her thin eyebrows arched. She knew I was up to something. Not so perfect.

Still, her carriage drove away and the butler let me in, telling me to wait while he fetched Miss Adele. I shivered with anxiety as I waited, the house feeling big and quiet all around me.

"What are you doing here?" Her voice drifted from the top of the curved stairwell. Adele descended, one hand on the polished railing. "I said you could ignore the invitation."

I pushed my shoulders back and recalled a Detective Rule about showing unwavering certainty even when in extreme doubt.

"I didn't come to socialize," I replied, my tone just as frosty as hers. "I came to discuss our *assignment*."

I hoped she understood my hidden meaning. Her butler stood just off to the side, waiting and listening.

She stopped on the bottom step. "Funny. I thought you said you'd be doing that assignment *solo*."

The butler flicked his eyes, trained to display only a lack of interest in me.

"I know, but I ended up finding so much information, I thought it might be better if I worked with someone."

Adele perked at this. "Did you?"

Her butler cleared his throat, apparently tired of our preamble. Honestly, so was I. Talking in code wasn't as fun as I always thought it would be.

"Shall I have Beatrice prepare a second supper to be sent up before I leave for the evening, Miss Adele?"

She waited an uncomfortable moment before replying. "I suppose so. Thank you, Gerald. Good night." She turned to go back up the steps and said to me from over her shoulder, "Come on, then."

She led me up to the second floor and down a short hallway.

"Where's your father?" I asked.

Adele hooked a left into a room. "The Copley. Hannah Grogan's having a —"

"Bon voyage dinner. I know. I was invited, too. But I told my grandmother I'd rather come here."

I followed her into the room. It was perfect: small, filled with books, large windows, and art on the walls and on stands around the room.

Adele got to the point quickly. "So what's this new information you suddenly have the urge to share with me? And it better be something substantial. I'll know if you try to feed me a bunch of fluff."

Adele perched herself on the edge of a seat cushion before the fire and waited, staring at me expectantly. My suspicions about Dr. Philbrick weren't exactly fluff, but they also weren't good enough all of a sudden. I didn't want to upset Adele or make her think I was holding back yet again. I did want to share what I knew with her. I'd shared it with Will, hadn't I? I could trust him. I wanted to trust Adele, too, and in that moment, I decided to give it a try.

"It isn't him."

Adele's smirk flew off her face. "Who?"

I was officially crazy. My uncle Bruce was going to be livid if this confession went south. But sometimes being a detective meant taking risks.

"Matthew Leighton. The Red Herring Heist mastermind," I answered. "My uncle's newest suspect isn't the person stealing your father's art."

The rain hadn't quit all day. Now it whipped against the windows. Adele screwed up the corner of her mouth.

"Why are you so certain of that?"

It wasn't a challenge. She was truly curious.

"Because you met him. He approached you on the dock after the second fire and came right out and told you that the art was being stolen. Why would he do that if he wanted to cover up the thefts with the arsons?"

Adele's lower lip dropped open. "*That* was *him*? But how do you know?"

I took out my notebook and flipped to the page where I'd noted the strange man's scent.

"You told me he smelled like musky soap, like wood. And then yesterday on Boston Common when I was next to Matthew Leighton, I noticed he smelled the same way — like strong piney soap."

Adele crooked her head to the side. "Are you finally going to tell me why you were there?"

I balled up my hand into my skirt. I didn't want to be afraid to tell Adele the truth. My family had hidden from the truth for so long, had lived in fear of it being discovered. I didn't want to be ashamed the way they'd all been.

"Because Matthew Leighton has been following me around Boston. My uncle thought he would be following me in the Common, too."

Of course, next Adele asked why a criminal would be following me.

"Because he's my —" But before I could finish my confession, the electric bulbs in the wall sconces and in the desk lamp behind us snapped out.

Adele gasped. Her face froze in alarm, her widened eyes lit only by the flickering flames in the hearth before us.

I got up to go to the window. "I'll see what the rest of the street looks like."

Veins of rain streaming down the glass cast the rest of the street into a blur, but there were definitely lights on in other homes.

"It's just us," I announced, turning around. Adele wasn't there. The door to the reading room was open and the last, ruffled folds of her dress were fluttering out into the hallway.

"Where are you going?" I asked, and hurried to catch up. I didn't relish the idea of staying in a dark, unfamiliar room alone.

Then again, it might have been preferable to the black hallway. I stopped just outside the reading room, unable to see a thing.

"Adele?" I said softly. Not yelling in the dark just seemed like a rule a person should never break, especially a detective.

"This way. Up the stairs." Her light footsteps padded up the carpeted steps to the third story. "Don't worry, it's just a power failure. My father has a hurricane lamp on his desk in the study. At the pace Beatrice walks, it will take her all night to get up to us with a light. Let's just get one ourselves."

I groped around for the banister and found it. "It's most likely a blown fuse. We should check the box in the cellar."

I had experience with fuse boxes now, after the

Cook case in July. Maxwell Cook and his son had cut off power to the hotel one night during a storm so they could —

I stopped midway up the stairs, the breath caught in my throat.

They'd cut off the power. During a storm.

"Adele?" I whispered. She was at the top of the stairs.

"What is it?"

I hesitated. I had no way to prove anyone had cut the power to the Horne house. There was no point in spouting off fearful theories.

"Nothing," I answered, and finished climbing the flight of steps. But I still felt uneasy.

The study was the second door to the left. Like every other room in the small mansion, it was completely dark. Adele made it to the desk and had the hurricane lamp in hand, but then the task of finding a matchbox daunted her.

"It has to be in one of these drawers," she said. I stood still as she rummaged around. The blackness felt thick and cold, like we would have to cut through it with sharp knives to see again rather than just light a match.

The shutters outside Mr. Horne's study rattled with the wind. As soon the racket stopped, I heard something else: The soft creak of the floorboards in the hallway.

"I think Beatrice was faster than you expected," I said.

Adele sighed, exasperated with her failed search for matches. "I should have brought the hearth matches from downstairs. Come on, we'll go get them."

But then a match flared, illuminating the face of a person standing in the doorway to the study. My heart spluttered and Adele screamed.

It wasn't Beatrice.

Chapter Fifteen

• • •

Detective Rule: In moments of severe distress and danger, a detective's most valuable possession becomes a very good hiding spot.

• • •

MATTHEW LEIGHTON HELD HIS INDEX FINGER to his lips in a gesture for us to hush. My jaw, and Adele's, hung open. Neither of us made a sound as he came inside the study and closed the door lightly behind him. But once he'd closed us off from the hallway, Adele straightened her back and the questions began.

"Who are you? What are you doing inside my house?" Her voice trembled, but she still jutted out her chin commandingly.

"You must forgive me, but I'm not accustomed to explaining to the resident of a home why I've broken in." He took his lit match to the desk and swept it over the lantern wick. The study brightened. He blew out the match. A gray tendril of smoke drifted in front of my grandfather's face. "But Suzanna can assure you I'm quite harmless."

Adele swung her shocked expression toward me. "You know him?"

I paused, choosing to look at him instead of Adele. "He's Matthew Leighton."

"The one your uncle is trying to arrest!" she exclaimed. "But this doesn't make any sense. Why can you assure me he's harmless?"

Leighton remained silent. He simply looked over to me, waiting to see how I would respond. He was giving me the choice, I realized. The choice to lie or to admit the truth. I wasn't going to lie.

I lifted my chin. "He's my grandfather."

The corner of Leighton's mouth twitched up with surprise. Adele gaped at me.

"Your   grandfather?" Adele's gray eyes narrowed into slits. "Your grandfather is the thief and you knew it? That's what you were keeping from me?"

"No! I mean, yes, I knew, but —" I saw the fury boiling up fast in her widened eyes. "He is not the thief, Adele! And he's certainly not an arsonist or murderer."

But I couldn't explain why he was inside her father's mansion. I turned toward him. "What are you doing here anyway?"

He walked out from behind the desk, still wearing his hat and coat, and even his gloves. It didn't look like he was planning to stay long.

"There isn't a lot of time to explain, Suzanna. I expect your uncle to be here very soon."

Adele and I glanced at each other as my grandfather moved to the floor-to-ceiling wall of shelves. Books packed every shelf.

"Why would he be coming here?" I asked. He inspected the titles, not turning around to look at me when he replied.

"I fear you've too quickly dismissed your uncle's competence. You know as well as I do how distasteful the idea of failing is to him. He failed apprehending me on the Common yesterday. Did you consider he might have a backup plan?"

He ran his hands along a row of leather spines — I wanted to know what he was searching the shelves for.

"But Uncle Bruce is supposed to be at the bon voyage dinner," I said as my grandfather came to the end of the shelves and to the stones of a cold, fireless hearth.

"Yes, as are you," my grandfather said, glancing over at Adele. "And you. But here the two of you are. Inside a house that was supposed to be empty all evening. Once again thwarting your uncle's plans."

Of course. Uncle Bruce had been planning on leaving the dinner party early, and then staking out the Horne house. For some reason, he believed Leighton would show up to take advantage of the empty house. But why? And how had Leighton known?

"If you know he's coming, why are you here? You're walking into his trap," I said.

Leighton bent down and peered inside the hearth. He stretched his arm inside and felt along the blackened inner walls of the fireplace.

"It's not his trap. It's mine. You see, a concerned neighbor sent in a complaint to the police station saying an old man had been seen prowling around the Horne house the last few nights. If I know Bruce's modus operandi — and I do, very well — I know that he will attend about an hour of this bon voyage dinner out of courtesy before slipping off to see if he might catch me in the act. He wants to trap the Horne art thief, and trap the thief he shall." He glanced back at me and propped up one eyebrow. "It just won't be the thief he's expecting."

As my grandfather ducked and entered the deep concave of the hearth, I couldn't help but marvel at his astute, clear thinking. He would have made a brilliant detective — that is, if he hadn't already been a thief.

"What are you doing?" Adele asked as Leighton's shoes scuffed through the old, cold debris on the hearth's stone floor. They brought up clouds of ash. There came an audible *click*, and then an entire panel of books beside the hearth — six shelves running at least six feet long — popped open like a door.

Adele stared in disbelief at the open panel. My grandfather reappeared, dusting off his shoulders and hat. He grabbed hold of the open panel door to what, I now realized, was one of Mr. Horne's hidden safes.

"How did you know about this safe?" Adele asked. From her dumbfounded expression, I deduced she had not.

Grandfather grinned and gestured to the wood floor. The bottom of the door ran flush along the floor, and now, looking closer, I saw an arc of scratches along the polished wood from the many times Mr. Horne must have opened the safe.

"I've taken a few unguided tours of your home before, Miss Horne." At Adele's widened eyes, Grandfather continued, "Don't be alarmed. I left everything in its original place."

I took another look at the scratched floors. My grandfather had the eyes of a detective as well. Perhaps that's what made him such a good thief.

Before I could look back up, my eyes traveled over the tips of Grandfather's black dress shoes. A silky layer of ash coated the shiny patent leather. Mr. Horne had come to Grandmother's dinner party with his shoes dusted in just the same way. He'd been taking care of some business, he'd told my uncle, but had avoided saying what about.

He'd also been elusive about something else: his collection's crown jewel. I was willing to bet it was right inside this secret safe. Mr. Horne must have gone to wherever it was being stored, extracted it, and moved it to his own home without telling a soul. All the while Detectives Snow and Grogan had been at the "club" waiting for him, as I recalled my uncle saying.

"Miss Horne." Leighton checked the hands of the mantel clock. Five minutes to eight. "It would be best if you and my granddaughter left the house now. Suzanna, hire a hackney back to your grandmother's house and stay there until everything your uncle and I have planned for tonight — separately, might I add — has unfolded. Quickly, girls."

"Don't!" she cried as Grandfather started to duck inside the safe. I was certain she'd figured out what was inside as well.

He stopped, but not because of Adele's plea. The floorboards had creaked in the hallway outside the study once again.

"He's arrived early," my grandfather whispered.

"Uncle Bruce?" I crossed the room and peered out the window. The rain had tapered off and I could see easier through the streaked glass. There was no one out front, though the statues of Hercules and the armless goddess made me take a second glance.

"No," my grandfather answered. "The real thief."

He'd followed me to the window and startled me now by shoving me behind the floor-length curtains.

"Make yourself invisible, Suzanna," he whispered, pulling the curtains farther along the rod to obscure me. He then hissed to Adele, "Miss Horne, hurry. Over here —"

Before he had the chance to finish, the study door squealed on its hinges.

Adele screamed yet again. I rolled my eyes, recalling my Detective Rule against that particular reaction.

"You! But you're . . . you're . . ." Adele stuttered.

I widened my eyes, though the only thing to see was the back of a thick panel of green velvet. But then the next voice made *me* want to scream.

"Dead. Yes, I know."

It was Detective Grogan. He was standing inside Mr. Horne's study. And he was totally and utterly alive.

Chapter Sixteen

• • •

Detective Rule: Prepare for the worst. Expect the unexpected. And don't count on backup.

• • •

I DIDN'T BELIEVE IN GHOSTS. I ALSO DIDN'T believe the dead could come back to life. So a more practical theory took shape in my mind as I stood behind the curtain: We'd all been fleeced like a bunch of ignorant lambs. Neil Grogan had faked his own death.

"I wondered if I might find you here, Leighton," Detective Grogan said blithely. I wanted to see him, not just hear his voice. I didn't understand why my grandfather had chosen to hide me this way.

"It seems I wasn't the only one who thought tonight would be an ideal time to see to the Degas," my grandfather replied.

My theory had been correct. It was inside the safe.

"I thought you'd gone the straight and narrow, old man," Grogan said. "You weren't much of a rival for the other artwork in Horne's collection."

Adele started to sputter off a shocked protest, but my grandfather interrupted.

"I suppose I've developed discriminating taste. And arson never was my cup of tea."

My heart thrummed wildly as my mind struggled to keep up. Grogan hadn't died. He was here, looking for the Degas, seeming to be on familiar terms with Matthew Leighton.

"I'd get off that pedestal if I were you," Grogan said, turning more somber. "I might have studied your methods, but not out of admiration. No. It was so I would know how to frame you for everything. You'll be taking the fall for all of it, Leighton. Consider it your debt to society. Hannah and I are happy to see you atone for your past sins."

I didn't want to believe it. Sweet, beautiful, grieving Hannah Grogan was an accomplice. And the bon voyage dinner had been a ploy. A way to entice Xavier Horne and Adele from their home, leaving it free and clear for Grogan. My grandfather had known it, too. He'd set everything up to keep Grogan in place until my uncle could find him.

"But you were sick," Adele said, still sounding confused. "We all saw you at my father's dinner. You couldn't have —"

"Sacrifices must be made to achieve your goals, Miss Horne. I ate a chili pepper before entering your father's party. Believe me, I *was* sick."

208

I recalled how he'd been sweating profusely. A whole chili pepper would set a person's throat and mouth on fire, for sure.

"But your body," Adele protested again. "They found it in the wreckage. It was buried in the cemetery!"

I heard Grogan chuckle. "They buried a body, yes, but not mine. It was a medical skeleton, actually."

A medical skeleton? Where on earth would he have gotten one of — I nearly gasped. Dr. Philbrick! He and Mr. Horne had been friends, a fellow art collector. Could he have trusted Dr. Philbrick with the Degas's whereabouts? Had Grogan and Dr. Philbrick been working together? And of course . . . he'd verified the remains of Neil Grogan. I'd just *known* Dr. Philbrick was a wretched man!

Adele suddenly whimpered, and the sounds of a brief struggle followed. I needed to see what was happening, but with my obstructed vision, the only thing I saw was the very edge of Mr. Horne's open wall safe. I revealed myself, what more could I possibly do? I could do more by making myself invisible, just as my grandfather had advised.

"Get the Degas, Leighton," Detective Grogan ordered. "I'll take it and be on my way."

"I know your plans for me," my grandfather said. "But what of Horne's daughter?"

There was a stretch of silence. I didn't dare even breathe.

"Miss Horne, finding you here has been quite a surprise. My wife told me you'd decided to attend her dinner party tonight," Grogan finally said. "It's unfortunate you chose not to."

Now I knew why Grandfather had shoved me behind this curtain. He'd done it to protect me.

"Harming a young girl isn't very sporting, Neil."

Grandfather sounded so conversational, as if he was suggesting Detective Grogan lessen the amount of salt he was sprinkling on his dinner.

"A young girl. An old man. It makes no difference to me." Grogan's cold reply sounded as if it had come from another person, not the quiet and intelligent Detective Grogan I'd known.

Coming within my restricted sight, my grandfather bent over and slipped inside the safe box. When he came back out, he had in his hand a small statue of a ballerina. The brown, waxy statue shimmered in the yellow lamplight. It was so basic and rough-looking. I couldn't believe this little statue was worth throwing away a career, dignity, and principle. Obviously, Detective Grogan did.

Horse hooves on pavement and the rattle of a carriage reached through the cold glass window at my back. Without moving the rest of my body, I turned my head so I could peer outside. There, pulled up along the curb, sat a dark carriage. I couldn't distinguish more than its box shape, but I knew who it must be. Uncle Bruce had arrived just as my grandfather had predicted.

"Set it on the desk," Neil Grogan instructed, apparently unaware of his partner's arrival.

For my grandfather to be following his orders, Detective Grogan must have had a weapon trained on Adele. Once he had the statue, what more would he need with my grandfather and Adele? They were liabilities. Let them go, and the police would be setting up a hunt for Neil and Hannah Grogan before dawn.

"Now, Miss Horne, I do hope you're not averse to small spaces," Grogan said, and then he was within my view, steering Adele straight inside her father's wall safe.

The heavy safe door with its shelves of books muffled her whimpering pleas as Grogan shut it. I stared at the back of his knee-length overcoat, at his head of fine, blond hair. When his profile came into view, I couldn't stop myself from feeling relief that he wasn't dead. Knowing he was a fraud ate into that relief a little bit. The small pistol in his gloved hand erased it altogether.

"And you, Leighton, are to lead the way downstairs. We have one last red herring to see to."

My stomach plummeted. The only red herring Grogan knew how to plant was fire. I had to get Adele out of the safe. She was already pounding on the inside of the door, but I had to give her credit: She wasn't yelling for me to help her. In fact, she'd done an admirable job pretending I wasn't in the study at all.

As soon as the room faded to blackness, and footsteps could be heard on the stairwell leading to the second floor, I pushed back the velvet curtain and raced to the deceiving shelves of books.

"Get me out of here!" Adele screamed. Her voice sounded like it was coming from underneath a stack of feather pillows.

I reached inside the cold hearth and ran my hands blindly over the stones. "Where's the handle?"

"I don't know!" Adele replied. "I didn't even know my father had a safe in here."

I ducked inside the deeply set fireplace, palms sweeping around flat against the rough stone. I needed to get downstairs and stop Detective Grogan from harming my grandfather.

Sweat beaded up on my back. I pounded my fist against the stone — and felt it sink inward. Dizzy with relief, I pushed it farther in, and *click*, the door to the safe popped open.

Adele rushed out, gasping for air. "I do happen to have an aversion to small spaces," she huffed. "As if he cared!"

I went to the window and peered out again. Uncle Bruce's carriage was still there, his driver sitting placidly in the box. I threw up the sash and leaned my head out into the cold, spitting rain.

"Up here!" I shouted, waving my hand over my head. The driver perked up and twisted his head up to the third-floor windows. "Send Detective Snow inside! Hurry!"

Adele and I then rushed into the black hallway.

"Where do you think they've gone?" she asked.

"Wherever Grogan can start a fire easily," I answered "Where does your father keep his spirits? Or the house's oil stores?"

The mention of fire propelled Adele forward. She beat me down the staircase.

"I think in the cellar," she answered. She grabbed my elbow as I passed her down the hallway. "No. This way, just in case."

She opened a door and dragged me into a closet. But then she was pulling me down a flight of steps — a servant stairwell. At the bottom, we jogged down a short corridor and then Adele stopped me. We'd come to another door. This one, I presumed, led to the kitchen. We pressed our ears to the wood and listened.

"We can't do anything until your uncle gets here," Adele whispered.

"Speak for yourself," I said, and grabbed for the knob. I was finished with hiding.

Inside the kitchen, a few candles sat flickering on the copper countertops. They seemed to have been lit for Beatrice's benefit. The old woman sat on a kitchen stool with her hands and ankles bound.

"Beatrice!" Adele went to her side and began scrabbling with the rope's knots.

"Miss Adele!" Beatrice gasped, her voice raspy. "I've seen a ghost! Detective Grogan came through here not two minutes ago."

"Did he do this to you?" Adele asked as the ropes around her ankles fell away. Looking closer, I saw what appeared to be a gag hanging loose around Beatrice's lace collar. Who had taken it out of her mouth?

"No, it was that other one who broke in about fifteen minutes before," she answered. Grandfather. Ashamed, I started in on the rope around her wrists.

"It wasn't a ghost," I told her. "Detective Grogan is alive. Where did he go?"

Beatrice nodded toward an open door next to a long wooden hutch filled with crystal and china. I started forward, but a hissing voice stopped me in my tracks.

"Suzanna? Suzanna!"

Adele, Beatrice, and I all swiveled toward the doors that led into the Hornes' dining room. The paneled kitchen door swung aside and Grandmother strolled in across the black and-white checkered tiles.

"Grandmother?" What on earth was she doing here? She was supposed to be at the Copley!

"There you are!" she exclaimed.

"Shhh!" Adele and I said in unison.

Grandmother balked at us. "I will not *shhh.* You hollered for us to come inside. Bruce took off running and then Will —"

I held up my hand to halt her. "Wait. Uncle Bruce already came inside? Where is he?"

Beatrice tapped my shoulder. "He went down into the cellar right after Detective Grogan."

A rash of cold gooseflesh prickled my entire body. Uncle Bruce must have been the one to free Beatrice of the gag. I stared at the open door to the cellar. Uncle Bruce was already down there with Grogan and Grandfather. There should have been shouting. There should have been a scuffle happening. But it was quiet. Too quiet.

I started for the cellar door, taking down a cast-iron frying pan from a pot rack as a makeshift weapon. "We need to help —"

But Detective Grogan appeared in the doorway, within an arm's length of me. He had his pistol in one hand and the Degas statue in the other. He shut the door with a kick of his foot.

"It's too late for help, Suzanna."

Grandmother screamed. I worried she'd keel over into another one of her fits, but she stood rigid, her look of astonishment fast turning to anger. The iron frying pan weighed heavy in my hand. My arm shook.

"You should have escaped while you had the chance," Grogan said to me.

Had he already lit the fire? The lamp oil and liquors, the wine and spirits were all down in the cellar with Grandfather and Uncle Bruce.

"Don't threaten my granddaughter, you despicable . . ." Grandmother sputtered as she searched for a piercing word. "Nincompoop!"

It was about as piercing as a blade of grass. First, Grogan chuckled at her choice of insult. But he then deepened his laughter. His shoulders shook with it. Four words streamed through my mind: *The element of surprise.* I brought the iron pan down as hard as I could on his hand holding the pistol.

The weapon clattered to the tiles and I kicked my foot out to knock it farther away. It spun underneath a butcher block and well out of his reach. Grogan broadsided me with his shoulder, pushing me to the floor. Abandoning the lost weapon, he darted toward the back kitchen door with the Degas clutched to his chest.

"Stop him!" Adele shouted, already running in pursuit.

Grogan threw open the back door, but another figure blocked the exit. Will! Grogan tried to shove past him, but Will put down his head and rammed into Grogan's chest as if he was a bull and Grogan was a red flag.

Grogan hit the floor, the back of his head smacking against the tile. I quickly opened the cellar door. A plume of thick smoke poured out, and with it stumbled Uncle Bruce. He staggered into the kitchen, a handkerchief pressed against his nose and mouth. Even in the dim light and through the cloying smoke, I could see an ugly red welt on his temple where Grogan must have hit him.

"Stay down, Neil," Uncle Bruce rasped as he walked unsteadily to Grogan's side.

Detective Grogan was trying to rise up from the floor, but he must have hit his head hard. He groaned as Uncle Bruce shoved him over and slapped on a pair of handcuffs. Once freed, the Degas statue rolled onto the floor and landed on its side. The *Little Dancer*'s outstretched leg and pointed toe lay reaching up into the air.

"How could you do this?" Uncle Bruce asked. Grogan didn't answer. I wasn't sure Uncle Bruce really wanted one right then anyway. In the last handful of minutes, he'd learned his partner had deceived him. Had made a fool of him. But at least Grogan had proved Matthew Leighton wasn't guilty. Well, not for this crime, anyway.

I turned back to the cellar door, expecting to see my grandfather hacking for air. He wasn't there.

"Where is Leighton?" I asked, a flutter of panic in my chest.

"Trying to put out the flames," my uncle answered, still coughing on the smoke. It was filling the kitchen fast and thick.

He heaved Grogan up from the floor. "Will, go to the telephone in the front hall and put a call in to the police station and then to the firehouse. Suzanna, fetch the Degas — my hands are full at the moment." He gave Grogan a thrust forward. "The rest of you, follow me."

Will rushed from the smoky kitchen, and Uncle Bruce and Neil Grogan followed. Grandmother and Beatrice, both coughing from the billows of smoke,

leaned against each other and started for the dining room.

"Suzanna, hurry. Come along," Grandmother called
back. I could barely see her, the smoke was so dense. It
had to be unbearable in the cellar.

"I have to go help him," I said, and started for the
door. Adele tried to pull me back, but I shrugged out of
her grasp.

"Zanna, you can't go down there." She grabbed my
arm once again.

"But he needs help!"

She pulled at me again. "Let's just get the Degas
and go!"

I yanked free, but even as Adele left my side, I was
squeezing back painful tears. My eyes were starting to
burn. My throat felt like it was swelling shut. I had
to get outside into fresh, clean air. But I couldn't leave
my grandfather behind when he'd gone so far to help
catch Detective Grogan. When he'd gone so far to protect me.

"Zanna!" Adele cried. "I can't find it. I can't find
my father's Degas! You've got to help me look."

"What?" I dropped to the floor where the smoke
wasn't as thick, and crawled to where Grogan had
crashed to the tiles. The *Little Dancer* hadn't rolled

more than two feet away from him. I swept my arms across the floor, connecting with Adele's as she frantically did the same.

"It's gone," I said, my eyes watering. But I could see the truth well enough.

There was only one kind of person who could have moved stealthily and silently through plumes of smoke in order to snatch it up.

A thief.

Chapter Seventeen

• • •

Detective Quote: "In order to be a realist, you must believe in miracles." — Henry Christopher Bailey

• • •

I DIDN'T WANT TO GO TO MISS DOUCETTE'S academy the next morning. Grandmother said I didn't have to, that it had been a long night and I was entitled to a day of rest. I also didn't want to see Adele. She hadn't said much after escaping her smoke-filled kitchen, but I knew she had to be angry. The fierce look she'd given me after I'd admitted Matthew Leighton was my grandfather had proved that guilt by association was nearly as bad as actual guilt. I didn't think I could handle another dose of it today.

But after less than ten minutes of lounging in bed beneath a thick duvet pulled up to my ears, I knew I'd end up driving myself mad if I didn't go to school. At least there I would be able to fill my head with French lessons and embroidery, with long division and elocution. I wouldn't have to think about my thieving grandfather or how gullible I'd been. I wouldn't have to think about how desperately I'd wanted him to have reformed, or how I'd selfishly believed he might change his ways now that he knew me. As if I had that kind of influence. As if I could change anyone that drastically.

I rang for Bertie and told her I'd need the carriage brought around after all. I then dressed quickly, the scratchy uniform providing a nice distraction. My braids were done hastily and probably looked that way, too, but I didn't care. I nabbed a slice of toast from the griddle in Margaret Mary's kitchen and stuffed it into my mouth before heading to the foyer.

"Is Grandmother doing better?" I asked Bertie as she held the cloak out for me.

Grandmother had been devastated to hear about Dr. Philbrick's involvement with Grogan. His illustrious career as Lawton Square's finest physician was officially at an end.

Bertie shook her head and opened the door for me. "I fear she's more upset about Dr. Philbrick than she is about Detective Grogan."

I agreed completely. The young doctor brought in by the police officers to check Grandmother's lungs last night had suffered the effects of her outrage. She'd taken in a little smoke, but despite her past breathing attacks, she had not had one after the fiasco at the

Horne house. To distract her and help the vexed doctor holding a stethoscope to her chest, I'd asked why she and Will had been with Uncle Bruce earlier that evening.

It seemed when my uncle got to the bon voyage dinner and realized Adele and I had stayed back at the Horne house, he'd tried to leave right away. My grandmother and Will had stopped him, knowing by the look on his face that something was wrong. He'd confessed to them about his trap for my grandfather, and they'd insisted on going with him to the Horne house. Thank goodness they had.

I said good-bye to Bertie and went outside. Grandmother's carriage was ready to go. The driver smiled at me, but I couldn't muster more than a disheartened hello.

Maybe I should have stayed in bed after all. Surely everyone at the academy would be attempting to cheer up Adele and me. Either that or barraging us with questions. Adele and her father had been able to stay in their home last night, the fire having been extinguished quickly as soon as the firemen had arrived. The kitchen and dining room had received little damage, but Mr. Horne and Adele had not cared one bit about that. It was the Degas they mourned. Not just for the value of it, but because it had been Adele's mother's favorite piece. Now it was gone, just like her mother. And my grandfather was to blame. How would Adele be able to look past that?

I climbed the short stack of steps into the carriage, and the driver shut the door as I was seating myself. A sharp, brief scream erupted from my throat as I saw a figure seated across from me on the opposite bench.

"Miss Snow?" the driver called through the door.

"I'm fine!" I answered quickly. I pressed a hand against my chest, my heart skipping beneath. "Grandfather, what are you doing here?"

Matthew Leighton leaned forward into the overcast morning light coming in through the street-side window. I noticed the curbside curtains were drawn. He hadn't wanted Grandmother peeking outside and seeing him. I'd ambushed my uncle in much the same fashion. Matthew Leighton certainly would make a fine detective, I thought with a shake of my head. What a shame he'd chosen the path he had.

"I didn't wish to leave things off the way I did last night," he replied.

I saw the welt on his jaw and the slant of his newly broken nose. Grogan's handiwork. The carriage jerked forward as the horses took a fast clip up Knight Street.

"Why did you even help us?" I asked. "Why did you bother to get involved if all you were going to do was steal something in the end?"

He hooked one ankle over a knee and threaded his fingers together, forming a tight fist. He looked toward his lap, not at me.

"I had my reasons for wanting to stop the person who was burning down those buildings and stealing the Hornes' art collection. They aren't noble, though, if that was what you had hoped to believe." He met my eyes now, his serious gaze unwavering. "I needed to clear my name, Suzanna. If my associates believed I was dipping into arson and murder, my contacts would fall off drastically. You might think the underground market is filled with thugs and good-for-nothings, but I've dealt with more titled, wealthy, respectable people than you could probably imagine."

I didn't want to imagine that anyone would be eager to purchase anything that had been stolen. It would never truly belong to them, no matter what price they'd paid.

"So you haven't changed," I whispered. "You'll never change."

He pursed his lips and blinked rapidly. I could tell he was uncomfortable.

"I have tried," he said quietly. The roll of the wheels and the cracking of the horses' hooves nearly overwhelmed his confession. "But I am afraid it's an addiction for me. I think I shall always be tempted."

Tempted to take what didn't belong to him. "But it's wrong, Grandfather. You have to know it is."

He continued to look gray and serious. "Suzanna, if you're to grow up to be a detective, you will fast learn that not everyone cares to always be *right*."

So some people just enjoyed doing bad things? I knew it was true. Why else would the world need police officers and detectives? There would always be crime and people doing things that were wrong. I just didn't want my grandfather to be one of them.

He stared at me, his shoulders rocking with the carriage's motion. A wistful grin lifted the corners of his lips. "I admire you, Suzanna. I wish . . ." He paused to think the rest of his sentence through. "I wish I could be more like my granddaughter."

Tears bit at my eyes. I had to look away, embarrassed my emotions had taken me by such surprise. He wanted to be like me? I didn't know if my tears had come because his wish had made me happy, or if it was because it had sounded so sad.

"How did you know I was coming to Boston?" I asked.

My grandfather sat forward on the edge of the bench seat. "Your mother. She wrote to me."

I sucked in a breath and nearly choked on it. "But . . . but she —"

"She has known my address for some time," he jumped in. "She asked me to keep my distance, but she wanted me to see you. I think she is very proud of you, Suzanna."

He reached into the inside pocket of his coat and took out a small, flat velvet box. "She has every right to be."

He placed the velvet box on the cushion beside me.

"It belonged to your grandmother. I gave it to her at our wedding," he said. I brushed the cover of the box with my fingertips before picking it up. "I would like for you to keep it. Your grandmother . . . well, she was very much like you."

I opened the box slowly. Inside, an amethyst cameo pendant sat nestled on a well-indented silk cushion. The cameo was of a woman with wild, flowing hair that wrapped around her neck and streamed out toward the edges of the oval pendant. It was beautiful.

I hoped it wasn't stolen.

"Thank you." I wanted to say more, but I couldn't. I knew what this cameo was. It was a parting gift. My grandfather was telling me good-bye.

The carriage slowed and the academy came into sight outside the window.

"And this . . ." My grandfather reached into the satchel beside him and brought out an object wrapped in linen. It was bulky and oddly shaped and I knew exactly what it was. In awe, I snapped the cover to the cameo box shut.

"Well, I suppose you know what to do with this," Grandfather said.

He handed me the object and when my fingers closed around it, I felt the thin leg of the *Little Dancer* pointed out in front of her, the hands she held clasped behind her at the small of her back. I let the linen unravel and fall onto my lap. It was the Degas.

"Why are you giving this back?" I asked.

The carriage had stopped. My grandfather had already opened the door on the street side of the carriage. He grabbed his satchel and leaped down onto the cobbles. He turned and looked inside at me sitting awkwardly with the rare *Little Dancer* statue in my hands.

"I suppose even thieves need to know what it feels like to do the right thing every now and again."

My grandfather winked at me, flashed a smile, and closed the door just as Grandmother's driver opened the opposite one. I sat immobile, my pulse galloping.

The police had apprehended Hannah Grogan the night before as her bon voyage dinner was ending and her trunks were being loaded into a carriage bound for the Anchor Line terminal. Inside her trunks, wrapped in clothing, had been all sixteen pieces of art thought to have been destroyed and stolen, including the Cézanne taken from Mr. Dashner — who, in the end, hadn't been criminally involved at all. Now, with the Degas, Adele and her father would have their entire collection restored.

"Miss Snow?" the driver said, still holding the door open. "Is everything all right?"

I looked over and spotted Adele passing by on the sidewalk behind him, surrounded by a throng of twittering academy girls.

"Adele!" I shouted. I didn't care how rude it was to shout for someone's attention, though the driver looked aghast.

Adele turned, her brows creased together as she peered inside the carriage. I thought to jump out with the statue, but didn't want to make too big a scene on the sidewalk with so many of the girls watching.

"What is it?" Adele asked.

I held up the statue, still grinning like an idiot. Adele squealed and flew past the stunned girls and

Grandmother's driver and inside the carriage. She landed on the bench beside me. I gave her the statue, her eyes wide with wonder and astonishment.

"Oh, Zanna," she breathed. "Oh, Zanna, thank you! How did you do it? How did you convince your grandfather to give it back?"

I picked up the ivory jewelry box and opened it so I could see the cameo again. I lifted the pendant from the cushion and felt its smooth backing. Flipping the pendant, I saw elegant cursive letters etched into the silver, rubbed dull in spots from the years the grandmother I had never known had proudly worn it.

With love and admiration,
M. L.

I ran my fingertips over the small letters. I knew my grandfather had intended the words for his wife, but I couldn't help but feel he now meant them for me as well.

"I didn't need to convince him," I answered.

Adele ran her hands all along the wax statue, inspecting it for damage. Even after everything it had been through the night before, there was none. Matthew Leighton was not a careless thief.

"Come on," I said. "Grandmother said she didn't mind my taking the day off from the academy. And I think your father will be just as thrilled to see that statue as you are."

Now it was Adele who couldn't stop grinning.

I glanced up at Grandmother's driver, who looked perplexed. "To June Street, please."

Adele and I sat back, side by side, each of us with a treasure in our laps. The carriage kicked forward and Adele grabbed my hand. She closed her palm around mine and squeezed.

About the Author

• • •

ANGIE FRAZIER IS THE AUTHOR OF *THE Midnight Tunnel: A Suzanna Snow Mystery* and the young adult novels *Everlasting* and *The Eternal Sea*. She lives with her husband and three daughters in southern New Hampshire. You can visit her online at www.angiefrazier.com.